Take me, she begged in her feverish mind.

And Jared did, his arm sweeping around her waist, plastering her against him as his other hand thrust through her hair. Then his mouth took hers, pleasuring it with a passion that excited her beyond anything she had known.

"Stay with me tonight." He breathed the words over Christabel's tingling lips, then lifted his head back from hers. "Look at me!" His eyes were like black coals, glowing at her. "Say yes, Christabel. Say you'll stay with me."

"Yes," she said, impelled by more than Jared would ever know to snatch this time from the life she had to lead. "I want this night with you, Jared."

One stolen night.

What harm could there be in it?

No harm…just pleasure…with the pleasure King.

And he kissed it would be.

Dear Reader,

Last year I chartered a plane to fly me from Broome, the pearling capital of the world, right across the Kimberly region of the great Australian outback. The vast plains are home to huge cattle stations, the earth holds rich minerals and the outposts of civilization are few and far between. I wondered how people coped, living in such isolated communities.

"They breed them big up here," my pilot said.
"It's no place for narrow minds, mean hearts or weak spirits. You take it on and make it work." He grinned at me. "And you fly. Can't do without a plane to cover the distances."

Yes, I thought. Big men. Kings of the outback. Making it work for them. And so the King family started to take shape in my mind—one brother mastering the land, running a legendary cattle station; one who mastered the outback with flight, providing an air-charter service; and one who mined its riches—pearls, gold, diamonds—selling them to the world.

Such men needed special women. Who would be their queens? I wondered. They have come to me one by one—women who match these men, women who bring love into their lives, soul mates in every sense.

In KINGS OF THE OUTBACK I have written three romances that encompass the timeless, primitive challenge of the Australian outback. Stories in the miniseries so far are: *The Cattle King's Mistress* and *The Playboy King's Wife*.

With love,

Emma Darcy

Emma Darcy

THE PLEASURE KING'S BRIDE

Kings of the Outback

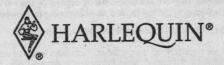

HARLEQUIN®

TORONTO • NEW YORK • LONDON
AMSTERDAM • PARIS • SYDNEY • HAMBURG
STOCKHOLM • ATHENS • TOKYO • MILAN • MADRID
PRAGUE • WARSAW • BUDAPEST • AUCKLAND

ISBN 0-373-12122-9

THE PLEASURE KING'S BRIDE

First North American Publication 2000.

Visit us at www.eHarlequin.com

Printed in U.S.A.

CHAPTER ONE

A MAN in a suit!

No-one wore a suit in Broome, especially not on a Sunday afternoon.

A surge of fear shot Christabel upright from the waist-deep water she'd been swimming in. She needed a better view of the man who was crossing the park above the beach, *wearing a suit!*

Was it one of *them*?

Had they tracked her down?

Before she could get a good look at him, his path took him behind the amenities block. She waited, her heart thumping wildly from the shock of being faced with the possibility that she had been found, despite all her precautions.

Six months she'd been here...perhaps, too long...long enough for her to start feeling safe...which was always a mistake. Stupid to ever feel *safe* from them, with so much at stake. Though there had seemed a very real chance of it, being so far away from everything that mattered to them, camped in this outpost of civilisation on the coastal edge of the great Australian outback.

Broome—a raggle-taggle, multicultural township that had grown up around the pearling industry when people still dived for pearl shell and died of the bends—was at the other end of the earth from the money men in Europe. Its history and tropical location, high on the west coast of the Kimberly region, attracted tourists, but *no-one wore a suit here*, not locals nor visitors. The heat alone demanded a minimum of clothing.

There he was again—just a glimpse of him crossing the open space between the amenities block and the cafe. His head was turned back towards the car park, making it impossible to identify him, but the suit said a lot to Christabel.

This was someone unprepared for the tropical climate.

Someone in too big a hurry to change his attire.

Someone who was heading purposefully for the caravan park that adjoined the beach area.

And *Alicia* had gone back to the caravan to fetch cans of cold drinks!

Sheer panic drove Christabel's legs to wade through the water in frantic haste. She ran through the shallows and along the damp sand, which gave her firmer footing until she could reach the rocky outcrop that led up to the camping reserve. If it was *one of them*, come to get Alicia, come to snatch her back to that other life...

No-o-o-o!

Christabel's mind burnt with fierce resolution as she leapt from rock to rock, every muscle tensing as she raced to fight for her daughter, determined on keeping her free from the nightmare world the money men would insist on constructing and maintaining. She would not let them take Alicia back to Europe. Never! Her daughter was safe *here*. If they'd just leave them alone...let them lead a normal life...

Onto the grassy bank of the reserve, her heart

pumping, feet pounding, her long wet hair whipping around her. People she'd come to know from neighbouring caravans called out, startled by her hurtling haste, but she couldn't pause, couldn't reply. First and foremost she had to reach Alicia before the man in the suit found her. Did he know where to look, which caravan they lived in? She couldn't see him but he had to be here somewhere.

Close now...she put on a last spurt, jumping over tent ropes and pegs, finally rounding the back of her van and...stopping dead.

He was there—the man in the suit—talking to her daughter, but he wasn't one of them.

It was Jared—her employer here in Broome, Jared King—nothing whatsoever to do with *them*!

And if she acknowledged the deep down truth, he was the main reason she'd stayed in this place, longer than she should have.

"Is something wrong?" he asked, frowning over her obvious state of agitation.

She leant against the side of the van, shaky with relief, one hand pressed to her wildly thumping heart, the other raking back the wet tangle of hair from her face. The dark, waist-length tresses undoubtedly looked like straggling ropes, the usual flow of waves in horrible kinks. It was embarrassing, having him see her like this, ungroomed, hopelessly discomposed and too nakedly vulnerable to successfully hide what had to stay hidden.

"Why were you running, Mummy?"

Having caught her breath, Christabel aimed what she hoped was a reassuring smile at her five-year-old daughter. "I thought you'd got lost."

Alicia huffed her indignation. "As if I would."

There she was, a delightful imp of a child, her lovely little face framed by a halo of brown curls, no fear at all in the big amber eyes, no shadow of repression hanging over her. Christabel was amazed at the happy self-assurance her daughter had developed here, in this Broome caravan park, and she was deeply grateful it was still in place.

"You were gone a long time and I was dying for a drink," Christabel offered in appeasement, conscious that Jared King was studying her quizzically and wishing he hadn't witnessed her fear. He was disturbingly perceptive at times and she simply couldn't afford to give too much away. Once people knew who she was, who her daughter was, everything changed.

"I've got them, see?" Alicia held up a string bag containing two cans of drinks. "I was on my way back…"

"I guess I should apologise for delaying her," Jared chimed in, holding up the can in his hand. "Alicia very kindly got me a cold drink, too."

"Why are you wearing a suit?" The accusatory words shot out of Christabel's mouth before she could stop them.

Another quizzical, more weighing look from Jared. In fact, his coat was off now, slung over one shoulder, and he'd loosened his tie and rolled up his shirt sleeves. The strong raw maleness that seemed to emanate from all three King brothers was coming at her in waves, making her acutely aware of being a woman.

"I mean it's so hot," she gabbled. "Ridiculous to

be walking around dressed like that. No wonder you wanted a drink.''

A slow, ironic smile. ''I must admit I'd rather be in a swimsuit.'' His eyes gliding over her appreciatively.

It wasn't a leer. Jared King wasn't the leering type. But she could feel his pleasure in seeing her like this, every curve hugged and outlined by the sleek yellow maillot, still wet from her swim, and his pleasure always did funny things to her, evoking a foolish happiness that muddled her mind and stirring physical reactions that left her miserably unsettled.

Her breasts were tingling right now, a shivery excitement running up and down her spine, her stomach turning mushy. If only he wasn't so handsome, so insidiously attractive to her in so many ways...

''Actually, I was driving home from the airport,'' he went on.

Of course! He was due home from his business trip to Hong Kong. She just hadn't connected the suit to Jared, but he would wear one to deal with the Chinese, commanding their respect on all levels. The pearl King, they called him, because he headed the pearling industry his family owned, but secretly Christabel had dubbed him the pleasure King. It was something in his eyes, a warm, caressing sensuality...

''Then I remembered my mother was away...''

His mother—Elizabeth King, of the sharp intelligence and shrewd judgment, a woman who'd lived too much and seen too much for Christabel to ever feel comfortable in her company.

''...no-one to talk to, wind down with...''

Making himself sound lonely, but there was never

any need for Jared King to be lonely, not a man like him. Or was he subtly tapping at her loneliness?

"…and I wondered if you might like to share my dinner and hear about your designs, the ones I took with me to Hong Kong."

His smile held a whimsical appeal, and there was a mocking challenge in his eyes over the bait he attached to the personal invitation. He didn't believe it would make any difference, but since she'd consistently refused to be with him in anything but a business situation, he was trying that angle…just to see her response to it.

"Did they like my jewellery?" she asked, feeling a surge of pride in the designs Jared had given her a free hand to create, and unable to deny her curiosity was piqued.

"Dinner?"

So tempting…strange how a man who always moved with such graceful elegance could exude so much male animal sexuality. He was tall and beautifully proportioned. His almost black hair tended to droop in a soft endearing wave over his forehead, but there was nothing really soft about his strongly boned face, except his rather full lower lip, lending his mouth the same sensual look she often caught in his dark brown eyes…eyes that were simmering at her now with promises of pleasure.

Christabel scooped in a deep breath, wishing she could indulge the desires he stirred in her. "No doubt you'll tell me everything at work tomorrow," she answered flatly.

"I was hoping for a pleasant evening together."

The tug to accept what he offered was stronger than

ever. But he would want too much, she told herself for the umpteenth time. Jared King was not the kind of man who would ever settle for less than everything he aimed for. Behind his quiet, affable demeanor was a will of steel she'd sensed many times.

"Vikki Chan invariably cooks a splendid homecoming dinner for me," he remarked persuasively, dropping in the fact that his Chinese housekeeper would be in the house—the sense of a chaperone. "I'm sure you'll enjoy it. In fact, her steamed fish is superb, well worth tasting."

Food wasn't the point, and he knew it.

"I like Chinese cooking," Alicia piped up.

Jared instantly dropped her a charming smile. "What's your favourite dish?"

"Honey prawns," came the decisive reply.

"Very tasty," he agreed with relish. "I'm sure Vikki would do some for you if your mother would like to bring you with her to my place for dinner this evening."

That was a hit below the belt, involving her daughter directly in the invitation. He'd never done it before and Christabel churned with resentment at the unfair ploy as both of them turned their gaze expectantly to her, Alicia's expression artlessly pleased at the promise of a treat.

"Can we go, Mummy?"

"I don't think so," she answered tersely.

The curt refusal bewildered her daughter, prompting the question, "Why not?"

"Yes...why not?" Jared echoed, maintaining a pleasantly invitational tone.

Christabel glared at him, hating the dilemma he put

her in. "Alicia eats early. She's in bed at eight o'clock."

"No problem." He glanced at his watch. "It's almost five now. If you come at six..."

"Stop it, Jared!" she burst out.

Slowly he raised his gaze to hers again and there was nothing the least bit affable in his eyes. They burned with the need to rip away every barrier she put up between them. They seared her soul with a truth she could not deny, the sure knowledge of the attraction she felt...the same attraction he felt.

"Some things can't be stopped, Christabel," he said quietly.

And she had no answer to that starkly honest statement.

Tension gripped her entire body as she fought the deeply personal needs he evoked. She wanted this man. She wanted to experience all of him so badly, it was like being torn in two, the rational part of her mind insisting an intimate involvement with him would spill over to an attachment with Alicia and the money men would never allow it, not in the long run, so it could only end in wretched torment.

Jared made one of his graceful gestures, the long artistic fingers opening in a curve of giving as he softly added, "Of course, the choice is yours."

What would it be like to have those fingers caressing her, making her feel loved and cherished and precious to him? Her stomach clenched in a savage desire to know how it would be...the pleasure King making love to her...to have this, just for herself, for at least a little time. Her heart drummed a vehement plea to make *her own choice*—a choice that shut out every other factor that had ruled her life for so many years.

"I'd like to go, Mummy."

And why shouldn't she? Christabel thought fiercely, looking at her daughter with an aching well of love. Why shouldn't Alicia enjoy the company of a man who didn't see her as a pawn in a monstrous web of greed? To add something more normal to their life here in Broome...why not?

"Then we shall go," she answered decisively, defying all the gremlins that rode on her shoulders.

Alicia clapped her hands in delight and lifted a gleeful face to Jared. "Honey prawns," she archly reminded him.

He laughed at her, his whole body visibly relaxing as he assured her, "I never go back on promises. Honey prawns there shall be."

"And chocolate chip ice-cream?"

"Alicia!" Christabel chided.

"I was just asking, Mummy," came the hasty justification.

"You know it's not good manners."

A doleful sigh. "Sorry."

Christabel sighed, too, afraid she was committing an act of utter madness on an impulse she would inevitably regret, yet when she lifted her gaze to Jared's and saw the happy warmth in his eyes, she couldn't bring herself to care about the consequences of her decision.

"Six-thirty would suit us better," she said, wanting time to dry her hair, time to feel all a woman's anticipation in the indulgence of getting ready for an evening with a man who truly wanted only *her*, not her connection to obscene wealth.

"Fine by me." He smiled the words, a smile that curled Christabel's toes.

"Thank you." Her voice came out husky, furred by emotions rushing free from the strictures of years of discipline.

"My pleasure," he replied, then transferred his smile to Alicia. "Chocolate chip?"

Her hands flew up into a fervent wish grasp. "Please?"

"I'll get some on my way home."

"Oh, thank you!"

He lifted his hand in a farewell salute to both of them, then strolled away with the air of a man who had come and conquered and the world was now his oyster.

Except it wasn't, Christabel thought ruefully. Only this little bit of the world belonged to Jared King. She remembered her visit to the great outback cattle station owned by his family, a vast land holding on the other side of the Kimberly from Broome. King's Eden, it was called. She'd been amongst the contingent of the family's employees in the pearl industry, invited to Nathan King's wedding, which had been an eerily soul-stirring ceremony, initiated by Aborigines playing didgeridoos.

She was glad she'd gone, glad she'd experienced such a unique insight into the traditions of the outback and the feeling of an ancient, timeless heritage that was tied to the land. Not the wealth made from it. The land itself. King's Eden.

Would she prove to be a serpent in Jared's Eden?

The carrier of evil that would poison his piece of paradise?

Sooner or later they would come—the powerful men in suits—and they'd destroy the normality of the life she'd established here, destroy whatever natural connections she'd made with people.

Christabel shivered.

Some things can't be stopped.

Jared's words...but they applied to much more than their feelings for each other. Still, for a little while...a defiant recklessness surged over the torturous fears...she *would* have what she wanted. And so would Jared.

It was *his* choice, too.

CHAPTER TWO

FEAR...because he'd been wearing a suit.

Jared mulled over that information as he drove back to the main shopping area to buy the chocolate chip ice-cream. It was another piece of the jigsaw he'd been fitting together ever since he'd met Christabel Valdez. The more he thought about it, the more it felt like a key piece.

His unexpected apparel had represented some kind of threat to her peace of mind. Was the suit simply an image that evoked bad memories, or was there more to it than that, a fear of someone who always wore suits turning up in her life again?

Jared didn't care for this last thought. Yet perhaps it tied in with her living in a caravan, a mobile trailer home she could take with her if she felt the need to move at a moment's notice. On the other hand, many people enjoyed the sense of a nomadic life that a caravan allowed. Not everyone wanted to put down roots in one place. Impossible to really know Christabel's truth until she chose to reveal it herself.

It wasn't the done thing to pry into the background of people who came to work in the Australian outback. There could be many reasons for dropping out of more sophisticated centres of civilisation. It might be as simple as a wish for a change of lifestyle, a need for space, a desire to experience something different...in which case they usually told you so. But

16

there were those who stayed silent, wanting to shed what they'd left behind...and that was their personal and private business, to be respected as such.

Christabel projected the first attitude but gave out so little of her past, Jared had concluded she wanted to shut the door on it. What had been tantalising, and intensely frustrating to him, was her stance of keeping everyone, including him, at arm's length, as though she couldn't bring herself to trust a close relationship, however much she might want it.

And she did want it with him.

Jared's fingers curled more tightly around the driving wheel as triumphant excitement coursed through him. At last he'd broken through her resistance. She'd given in. Though why now...he shook his head. It didn't matter.

Perhaps it was the realisation that her fear—whatever its cause—was unfounded with him. If so, all the better. He didn't want fear to play any part in their relationship. He'd sort that out soon enough, now he had the chance to get close to her, closer than he ever had before in five long months of laying subtle siege to her defences.

Christabel...

He smiled on a wave of sheer exhilaration as he rolled the lovely lilt of her name through his mind...a name he'd thought might haunt him all his days, accompanied by a vision of eyes that glittered like gold in moments of fierce emotion and darkened to a simmering, sensual amber in moments of pleasure.

A woman with the heart of a tiger, he'd often thought, imagining her stretched out on his bed, lazily slumbrous, yet with those eyes inviting dangerous play, her satin-smooth olive skin gleaming, the rich abundance of her glorious long hair spreading silkily across pillows, the soft, perfect femininity of her body calling to everything male in him, a beautiful exotic mystery.

A haunting name, a haunting image...and all this time it had seemed the reality of her might remain forever elusive.

No more.

Tonight she would be within his reach.

Tonight...

It took considerable effort to bank down the passion she stirred in him and concentrate on practical details. Even his fingers were tingling as he activated the car phone and pressed his home number.

"Vikki here," came the familiar sing-song voice.

"Visitors for dinner, Vikki. Christabel Valdez and her daughter." It gave him intense pleasure to say that.

"Ah! So you win. I said to your mother, Jared will win. He does not know how to lose, that boy. He keeps at it until he wins."

He laughed. Vikki Chan had been with the family all his life, cook and housekeeper to his widowed grandfather, staying on to maintain the old Picard home for his mother after Angus Picard's death. It wasn't the least bit surprising she knew of his interest in Christabel. Jared suspected she knew everything that went on in Broome from her many long-established grapevines. Besides, his mother was in the habit of confiding worries to her.

"I'm about to pick up the ice-cream her daughter

likes," he informed. "I also promised Alicia honey prawns…"

"No problem. I shall call and have the best green prawns delivered. Also more fish. Is fish all right for your Christabel?"

His Christabel…he hoped. "I'm sure it will be perfect. They'll be arriving early. Six-thirty. Alicia goes to bed at eight."

"I will take care of the little one. A bedroom near mine."

"They may not stay beyond eight, Vikki." He couldn't assume too much, given the hot flare of resentment from Christabel when he had used Alicia to press the invitation. In fact, the giving in may not extend anywhere near as far as he wanted.

"I shall work it so you have time alone with her, Jared," came the arch reply. "I have not lost my touch with children. And I very much doubt you have lost your touch for winning."

Her confidence set him smiling again. "You're a wicked old woman, Vikki Chan."

He heard her cackling with delighted amusement as she disconnected to make other calls and imagined her wizened little face creased into a myriad happy wrinkles and her black eyes asparkle with plots and plans.

Vikki Chan would never say how old she was. Probably in her eighties, Jared guessed, though still incredibly spry and full of a zest for life. She'd be on the telephone right now to her seafood supplier, demanding the very best and threatening terrible fates if it wasn't delivered. The pencil she invariably poked through the bun that kept her scraggly grey hair under tight control would be down in her hand, making notes no one else could read.

Chinese, she said, but Jared had learnt to speak and read Chinese proficiently and he could never decipher what she wrote. It gave Vikki an enormously smug pleasure to keep her little secrets, while worming out everyone else's. Though not even she had managed to learn anything about Christabel beyond what Jared had learnt himself.

Which wasn't much.

She knew Amsterdam. A conversation on diamonds had dropped that fact. Singapore was another piece of the jigsaw, perhaps simply a stopover on her way to Australia. Wherever she had learnt it, she had an extensive knowledge of jewellery and a keen appreciation of how it was valued.

He parked the car in Carnarvon Street, crossed the road to Cocos Ice Cream Parlour, bought two individual tubs of chocolate chip for good measure since Christabel might like it, too, plus several cones in case licking was preferred to spooning.

From there it was a short drive up to the bluff where the old Picard home overlooked Roebuck Bay. Prime position, Jared always thought appreciatively, though the house itself was not a particularly impressive place, just a big, rather ramshackle wooden building, surrounded on three sides by wide verandas that could be shuttered against inclement weather.

Still, it held a lot of history for his mother and it was large enough to accommodate the whole family with space to spare whenever his brothers came to Broome. Tonight it was going to accommodate Christabel Valdez and her daughter, for as long as they were willing to stay. *As long as he could make it,* Jared privately vowed as he headed inside to the kitchen with the ice-cream supplies.

Vikki was chopping vegetables at her workbench. "Everything okay?" he asked, crossing to the freezer.

"Of course." She eyed him critically. "You look very hot, shirt sticking to your back. You need a shower and a shave."

Having put the ice-cream away, he placed the cones on the bench and shot Vikki a teasing grin. "I think I can remember to brush my teeth."

Unabashed, she returned an arch look. "That cologne you have…it is very nice. Definitely a subtle come-on."

"I'm glad you approve my choice. Been sniffing it, have you?"

She humphed. "You need all the help you can get to make the most of this night."

"Not artificial help. It won't impress Christabel one bit. Nothing has…not who I am or what I am or any material advantages she could get from me."

"Maybe…maybe not. I'm thinking a clever woman doles out a long rope for a man to hang himself with. You are a prize, Jared, and it occurs to me no other woman has ever tied you up this firmly."

He shook his head. "She doesn't see me as a prize. That's not where it's at."

She raised derisive eyes. "The executive head of Picard Pearls? A man with his own custom-fitted Learjet? One of the Kings of the Kimberly?"

"It's all irrelevant to her. I'd know if it wasn't. I'm not a fool, Vikki."

"Men in love can be blind."

"Not that blind."

There was a loud rap on the back door. "Ah, the prawns and the fish!" Vikki made a shooing gesture as she moved to answer the summons. "Go off with you, Jared. And if you want my opinion, if your Christabel doesn't know you are a prize, *she* is a fool."

Not a fool, Jared thought, leaving the kitchen to go to the suite of rooms he'd made his. Christabel operated on values that had nothing to do with wealth. That had been clear to him from the beginning, and her independent stance had remained consistent ever since. This was a woman who thought for herself, acted for herself and was wary of allowing any outside influence into her life.

He dumped his briefcase in his home office, stripped off in his bedroom and moved automatically towards showering and shaving, his mind occupied with memories....

The necklace...looking up from the paperwork on his desk and seeing it around his secretary's throat...

"Where did you get that piece of jewellery?"

"Oh, sorry!" A fluster of guilty embarrassment. "I know I should be wearing pearls..."

"It's all right. I just want to know. The design is very striking." Artistic, elegant, cleverly leading the eye to the enamelled pieces it featured.

"Yes. I love it and couldn't resist buying it."

"Where from?"

"At the Town Beach markets on Friday night."

"The markets?" It was not market goods. It was class. High class!

"Yes. Usually there's only cheap, fairly tacky stuff, but there was this rather small collection of re-ally super costume jewellery on the stall that sells velvet jewellery bags. I would have bought more but this was seventy dollars."

"Locally made?"

"Well, the person who made it is a newcomer, though she's been here a while now. Lives in the caravan park. Very exotic-looking. Comes from Brazil, someone said."

Exotic…he'd imagined some over made up woman in a multicoloured floating garment…yet that design had tugged him into reconnoitring the market stalls at Town Beach the following Friday evening.

His first sight of her…like a magnet pulling him, his heart hammering, pulse racing. She'd been chatting to her co-stall holder. Had she *felt* him coming? Her head turned sharply. Their eyes met. An instant sexual awareness. Electric. How long had it lasted? Several seconds? Then she stiffened as though suddenly alert to danger, and her lashes swept down, shutting him out.

The abrupt switch off paused Jared in his tracks. It was wrong, unnatural. He sensed a shielding that was determined on blocking him out, and the urge to fight it welled up in him. She didn't know him, he realised, and he didn't know her. He tempered his more aggressive instincts, listening to the one warning him that storming defences was not a winning move.

He slowed his approach and made a casual study of the jewellery on the trestle table she stood behind. Each piece, to his eye, was a unique design, displaying a creative artistry he found almost as exciting as the woman. Part of her, he thought, an intrinsic part of heart, soul and mind woven into patterns and fashioned with exquisite taste. He couldn't resist touching them.

"You made these?"

Her lashes lifted. "Yes." She stood very still, her eyes alert, reminding him of a cat's, watching what his next move would be.

He smiled. "Your own designs?"

"Yes." No smile in response. A waiting tension emanating from her. "Are you interested in buying?"

She wanted him gone, which seemed so perverse it intrigued Jared even more. "You must have had training," he remarked.

She shrugged. "I am now self-employed. Do you wish to buy?"

"You come from Brazil, I'm told. Perhaps you worked with H. Stern in Rio de Janeiro?"

More tension. A flat-eyed stare. "Why are you inquiring about me? Who are you?"

"Jared King. I head the Picard Pearl Company here in Broome. I've been looking for someone. Someone special. You...I think."

A flare of alarm...recoil in her eyes.

The personal element was backfiring on him. He instantly slid into business. "I want a unique range of jewellery designed, featuring our pearls. I think you might be the right person to do it."

No hesitation, not the slightest pause or flicker of interest. "I am not the person you want, Mr. King."

"I think I should be the judge of what I want," he dryly returned.

"And *I* the judge of what *I* want," came the sharp retort.

"It could be worth your while…"

"No," she cut in firmly. "I am self-employed. I like it that way. Now, if you're not interested in purchasing…"

"I'll take the lot."

That startled her. But after the initial shocked flash of disbelief came a hard-eyed challenge. "It will not buy you anything but this jewellery, Mr. King."

"I didn't imagine it would, Miss…?"

Her mouth visibly thinned, wanting to hold it back from him, but her own intelligence told her it was too easily learnt from others here. "Valdez," she answered tersely.

He fished out his wallet. "How much?"

She noted down the prices as she wrapped each piece in individual sheets of tissue paper, then added up the total and showed him so he could check it himself.

As he paid her, he also handed her a business card. "I am seriously interested in your talent as a designer," he pressed quietly. "Please…think it over. Check my credentials. My contact numbers are on that card."

"Thank you," she said stiffly and gave him nothing more than the plastic bag in which she'd placed the tissue packets.

Having been comprehensively dismissed, he knew nothing would be gained by staying, but he left determined to seek her out again if she didn't come to him.

Two weeks he gave her, more than enough time to

check him out and consider the possibilities and advantages in the situation. Not the slightest nibble of interest from her. Nothing.

He did the pursuing and every meeting he managed was fraught with tension, her determination not to form any connection with him conflicting with the pull of an attraction she struggled to deny. It took a month of persistent angling and negotiation to get her to agree to submit designs that he could buy from her as he wished. Even then she kept her involvement with him strictly professional, continually blocking any encroachment on her private life.

Dancing with her at Nathan's wedding...the intense pleasure of finally holding her in his arms, though not nearly as intimately as he wanted, her hands pressing a resistance to full body contact.

"Are you enjoying your visit to King's Eden?"

She smiled, relaxing but still maintaining a wary distance. "Very much. It is what one might call a revelation. A world unto itself."

For once, her beautiful face was lit with fascinating animation as she listed her impressions of what she'd seen and felt throughout this outback experience. The flow of glowingly positive comments fuelled Jared's hope that she could be drawn into his life, could be happy belonging to it.

"And now you've met all my family," he prompted, wanting some hint of how she felt about them.

An enigmatic smile. "Yes. Your mother must be very proud of her three sons. And pleased with Nathan's marriage."

It was more an objective observation than a personal comment, frustrating Jared's purpose again. "What of your own family, Christabel?"

A slight twist to her smile. "I do not belong to anyone but my daughter." A gleam of warning in her eyes. "It suits me that way."

"You could have brought her with you this weekend." In fact, it was strange she had not, given how watchful and protective she was of the child.

A slight shake of her head. "The family she is staying with is safe. I know them from the markets. Good people. Long-time local residents of Broome."

"So you *wanted* to come alone."

A mocking gleam. "I simply wanted my curiosity satisfied, Jared. Don't make any more of it than that."

"And is your curiosity...completely satisfied?" he challenged, acutely aware of his own burning need for all she withheld from him.

She shrugged. "How can I fully know a legend I haven't lived? The Kings of the Kimberly...a hundred years of building what you have here and in Broome. I cannot expect to grasp more than a glimmering of what it comprehends."

The evasive answer pushed him into asking, "Do you find the idea of long roots inhibiting?"

She raised her eyebrows. "Have you found it inhibiting?"

"No."

"It is very much part of you, isn't it?" More a statement than a question.

"Yes."

"So you should stay happy with your life."

The wry resignation in her voice stirred a deep well

of frustration. Why was she keeping herself separate from him? Why couldn't she let the attraction between them follow its natural course?

"Is anyone completely happy without a partner to share their life with?" he demanded tersely, nodding to the bride and groom dancing together, just a few metres away from them. "Look at Miranda. Look at Nathan. *That is happiness*, Christabel! Can you not imagine that…want that…for yourself?"

He caught a glimpse of raw yearning on her face as she looked at his brother and the woman he had just married. For several moments an air of sadness hovered around her. Then she turned her gaze back to him and her eyes were flat, hard. "I've been married, Jared. My husband is dead but I still live with him. I will always live with him."

"He's dead, Christabel. Dead is dead," he countered harshly, unable to stop himself, feeling her vibrant vitality, the pulsing sexuality that aroused his so strongly.

"Believe me…" Her eyes bitterly derided his claim. "…you would not want to live in his shadow."

He didn't believe her.

She wasn't a woman in grief.

He'd witnessed his mother's grief after his father's death. Christabel Valdez did not want her husband back. She wanted *him*, and be damned if he'd be driven away by a shadow.

Jared wiped the few remaining bits of shaving cream from his face and grimaced at the hard ruthlessness in the eyes reflected in the mirror. He'd been thinking,

Nothing was going to come between him and Christabel Valdez tonight! But, of course, she would have her daughter with her, the daughter of the man she'd married.

He'd used the child.

Christabel may very well use her, too.

But he did have Vikki Chan on his side.

He smiled as he tossed the towel aside and picked up the bottle of cologne—Platinum Egoiste by Chanel. He might as well use every bit of ammunition he had in this war, because war it was. And he was sick to death of fighting shadows. He wanted hands-on combat. Action.

His body stirred in anticipation.

Vikki was right.

He *would* keep at it until he won.

CHAPTER THREE

CHRISTABEL parked her four-wheel drive Cherokee at the end of the street that ran parallel to the old Picard property. There was no road in front of it, nothing to disturb the view it commanded over Roebuck Bay. The house itself was considered a historic landmark, built by Captain Trevor Picard in 1919, the owner of forty pearling luggers—so she'd read in the museum records.

This was where Jared lived.

He was in there waiting for her.

Christabel's fingers stayed tightly curled around the steering wheel as she tried to steady her nerves. Ever since she'd accepted his invitation she'd been defying all the things she'd forbidden herself, wanting what he wanted, wanting to show him she did. She was twenty-seven years old and she'd never had a lover, only a husband who'd only ever cared about his own pleasure, never hers. She was sure Jared would be different.

"Is this it, Mummy?"

"Yes." This was definitely *it*, Christabel decided as she answered her daughter.

"Then why aren't we getting out?"

"Getting out now," she answered.

Alighting from the driver's seat and rounding the Cherokee to the passenger side, Christabel found her gaze drawn to the house where Jared chose to live. It was a big, solid old place. Other people with the accumulated wealth of the King Picard family might have torn it down and built something grander, more modern and impressive, and it would have meant nothing but a symbol of wealth.

Like the majestic old homestead she'd seen at King's Eden, this house seemed to stand for endurance, for something lasting beyond any one person's life and death.

It had been caringly maintained—the building, the garden. Caring...everywhere she looked...the precise paintwork on the house, the neatly trimmed bougainvillea, the lustrous clumps of ferns and tropical foliage...and the sharp realisation came that what was in front of her stood for things she could never share with Jared and what she was setting out to do was wrong.

Too wrong to go on with.

She shouldn't have accepted this invitation, shouldn't be here. Jared King was too good a man to be used and left, as though he was not worth more than a strictly lustful affair. Maybe that would be enough for him...but what if it wasn't?

She stopped by the passenger door. Alicia was making an impatient face at her through the window. Should she get back in the Cherokee and drive away? How could she explain that to her daughter—such bad manners? Impossible. Yet to go ahead, dressed as she was...it was a tease, a deliberate sexual tease, meant to signal her willingness to end the torment of wanting. Jared would notice.

And she'd burn with embarrassment at the rampant wantonness that had led her into presenting such a provocative invitation to satisfy every physical desire they'd stirred in each other.

Alicia knocked on the window. "Come on, Mummy."

She'd have to minimise the effect. Somehow. And leave as soon as she decently could. It had been wrong to give in to this…this raging temptation. She must never do it again. It wasn't fair to him. He was wasting his time with her, time better spent looking for a woman who could embrace all that his life meant to him.

Best to break the connection after tonight. Or limit it more than she already had, make Jared understand it was not to be. Maybe she could lead into that this evening.

Taking a deep breath to calm the inner flood of agitation, she opened the door and released Alicia from her seat belt, glad she had her daughter to come between her and Jared and determined now not to accept any offer of a bed for Alicia when eight o'clock came. No time alone with him. She couldn't risk it.

"Big trees, aren't they, Mummy?" Alicia commented, looking up at them as Christabel lifted her out of the vehicle.

"Older than any others in Broome, I'd imagine," she replied, struggling for an air of normality as she, too, looked up at them.

The native gum trees had been planted in a row along this side of the house, just within the white picket fence that surrounded the property. The width of their huge white and grey trunks and the spread of the branches testified to the number of years they had stood, while undoubtedly other such trees had been cut down in the past to provide building materials for the township. They were also a testament to a family who looked after what they had, who valued deep roots, who were given to *long-term commitment* as naturally as they breathed.

"I like this place," Alicia declared, happily taking Christabel's hand for the walk around to the front gate.

Her little face beamed excited anticipation and excess energy poured into an occasional skip to her step, making Christabel smile over the uninhibited pleasure being so naturally expressed. Alicia looked very cute in a lime green shift she'd selected herself from a hanging rack at the markets, and simple little sandals with seashells sewn on the straps. To Christabel's mind, it was much better for her daughter not to be a designer-clad little miss, filled with a pompous sense of her own importance.

She wished her own appearance was as artless, acutely aware that the cotton-knit weave of her dress clung to her curves before flaring into a flirty little skirt that ended mid-thigh. It was definitely a sexy garment, sleeveless, its low round neckline dipping to the swell of her breasts. She wore no bra and only a minimal G-string, not wanting to break the slinky feel of the soft fabric. Its dark red colour hid the nakedness underneath, but the obvious shape of her breasts and the smooth line of hip and thigh suggested it.

Despite the heat, she had left her hair down, readily touchable, rippling around her shoulders in a loose fall to her waist. Her bare feet were slipped into black strappy sandals, easily slipped out of, as well. On a black leather thong around her neck hung a copper sun disk, split in two and joined by a crescent moon from which dangled uneven strings of triangles—all in copper, which had swirls of dark red through its polished surface. It was her own design and she liked the elemental nature of it.

She had been feeling very elemental as she had chosen what to wear...*and not wear*. It was what she had wanted to feel, a woman meeting a man, intent on revelling in the most basic level there was between them. Totally pagan and primitive, she'd told herself on a wave of mad exultation, indulging the wicked sense of throwing all caution to the winds and having what she wanted, regardless of consequences.

It was only too easy to fool herself into believing she had a right to this. The right of a woman. Being a mother should not mean she had to suppress her own sexuality, and she had never wanted a man as much as she wanted Jared King.

"Looks like a storm coming, Mummy."

Jolted from her intense inner reverie, Christabel looked out over Roebuck Bay. Black clouds were looming ominously above the horizon. No romantic moonrise tonight, she thought wryly. Not that she'd come for romance. In fact, a quick tropical storm was more in keeping with the kind of relationship she'd envisaged with Jared...a storm that would blow over and just be a part of the past when she moved on.

Could it be so?

Was she worrying needlessly?

Or would it leave wreckage in its wake?

"We'd better get inside before it starts," she said,

quickening her pace, aware of how swiftly storms swept in here.

"Can we watch it from the veranda?" Alicia asked eagerly, always fascinated by the lightning show that usually preceded the deluge of heavy rain. She'd seen quite a lot of it this summer, although it wasn't called summer here. It was simply the wet season and the rest of the year was the dry. The lightning was always spectacular, and Alicia found it more exciting than frightening.

"I guess so," she answered, reasoning Jared would want to please her daughter, given his ready offer of honey prawns and chocolate chip ice-cream.

They arrived at the front gate. Christabel reached over it to work the catch on the other side. To her frustration, it seemed to be stuck. She released Alicia's hand to give herself leverage for a stronger tug, even while thinking this physical obstacle was a sign she was trespassing where she shouldn't go. The gate didn't want to let her in. It was protecting the people it was built to protect.

"I'll open it for you!"

She looked up to see Jared emerging from the veranda, already descending the steps to the path leading to the gate.

"It's probably stuck, not having been opened since the fence was last painted," he explained, striding towards her. "We mostly use the side entrance."

His white shirt was unbuttoned, flapping open as he walked, revealing black curls nestled on his darkly tanned chest and a fine line of hair arrowing down, disappearing below the belt line of white shorts. Snug, sexy shorts, leaving most of his muscular legs bare.

His flagrant maleness caught the breath in Christabel's throat. She barely had wits enough to withdraw her hand and stand back from the gate for him to work the catch free for her. The urge to simply feast her eyes on him was so strong, it was difficult to think of anything else.

His thick dark hair looked soft and springy, newly washed. He had neat ears for a man, tucked close to his head. His jaw was shiny-smooth. She picked up a tantalising scent, something sharper than fresh sea air, intriguingly attractive, multi-layered in essence. Very Jared, offering sensory pleasure.

"There!" He beamed a triumphant grin at them as he swung the gate wide.

"Thank you," Alicia piped up, minding her manners.

"You're welcome," he returned, waving them forward, his eyes gathering a gleam of more personal triumph as his gaze travelled from her daughter to Christabel herself.

"Lucky you arrived before the storm," he remarked. "I was about to close the shutters on the veranda."

"We like storms," Alicia informed him.

"Well, in that case, we'll leave the shutters open unless the rain starts coming in."

Happy with this indulgence, Alicia skipped ahead along the path. Christabel waited for Jared to shut the gate behind them, inwardly churning over what he had to be thinking, given the overt provocation of her dress. She couldn't bring herself to walk ahead, knowing she would feel him watching the free movement of her buttocks with every step she took. It wouldn't be so bad, walking with him.

His shoulder muscles bunched as he realigned the catch and fastened it. Her own tautly strung nerves thrummed with the tension coming from him, causing her stomach to contract and sending little quivers down her thighs. Yet when he turned to her, it was with a warm, welcoming smile, aimed at relaxing any fears she might have over accepting his invitation.

"I like the pendant you're wearing. Very eye-catching," he remarked.

"It goes with the dress," she answered before she could catch the words back.

To her intense relief his gaze didn't wander downwards. His eyes twinkled appreciation straight into hers. "Once again you demonstrate your talent for the perfect touch."

"I'm a long way from perfect, Jared," she blurted out, guiltily conscious of raising expectations she didn't know if she could meet or not. Would he want more from her than having his desire sated? Was it just a physical craving for him?

"You gave me the kind of showcase I wanted for our pearls, Christabel. Your designs are now on display in Hong Kong, exciting far more interest in the trade than a showing of our wholesale product."

A rush of pleasure eased her sense of guilt. "Then I've given you something of value for all the time you've spent on me."

He frowned quizzically. "I do want more."

The quiet tone carried a wealth of suggestion, tapping straight into the pulsing core of why she'd come, why he'd invited her. He wanted more and so did she, and it had nothing to do with pearls and professional business. She stared at him, feeling the gathering ache of need he stirred, wishing it could be appeased, wondering if the risk would be worth taking.

"It must mean something to you, as well," Jared went on, "knowing your creative vision has excited such interest?"

It was on the tip of her tongue to say, *I only did it for you,* but that was far too revealing a truth. "I simply enjoy designing, Jared. What you do with my work…that's your business. It doesn't relate to me any more."

"But you could make a real name for yourself," he pointed out.

A kick of alarm hit her heart. "You didn't use my name, did you?"

His frown deepened. "No. As per our agreement, the jewellery was simply labelled Designs by Picard. But I do feel very strongly that you should get recognition, Christabel."

She shook her head, the anxious moment receding at his reassurance. "I truly don't want that."

"Why not?"

Because they'll find me through you. But she couldn't say that. Dragging him into her dilemma wouldn't solve anything. "I'm happier this way."

"You could make a very substantial career."

"I don't need a career. What I need is to be free, Jared. Can you understand that?" A kind of desperate panic welled up in her, forcing an explanation that warned him where she stood. "Not to be tied down. Not to be owned. Not to have my life ordered by others. So don't count on more from me. Don't ever count on more. I've tried to tell you...."

"Yes, you have," he agreed. "I'm sorry if you think I haven't respected those feelings."

The passionate outpouring broke into a ragged sigh. "Then why am I here?" she muttered defeatedly.

"Because it's where you want to be."

As simple as that. Except nothing was really as simple as that. She looked at him in anguished uncertainty.

"Let it rest for now, Christabel. Come..." He gestured towards the veranda, smiling in light whimsy. "...it's only one evening."

One evening...he was right. It involved only a short time span. Nothing need happen that she didn't want to happen. And Alicia was with her.

Her gaze automatically swung to the veranda as she fell into step beside Jared. Alicia was chatting to a little old woman who was bent over, exuding interest in what the child was saying.

"Vikki Chan," Jared elucidated. "Probably checking when and where to serve the honey prawns."

As with many of the Chinese population in Broome, she wore loose cotton trousers and an overblouse with slits on the side. Her grey hair was scraped into a bun and her much wrinkled face was creased into an indulgent smile. Clearly Alicia was at ease with her.

Christabel gratefully seized on an impersonal topic of conversation. "I find it amazing that the Chinese and Japanese people here have adopted Western society names."

"They've been here a long time. Descendants of the divers in the old days."

"Yes, but they still keep many of their customs. Like leaving money on the graves in their cemetery."

"Ah, but that has to do with beliefs, not day-to-day mixing with people. The captains of the pearling luggers gave Western names to their divers, for their own convenience in identifying them. The practice was accepted and passed on."

"A very arrogant practice, imposing one culture on another."

"Not a culture. Just a name. The Chinese culture is alive and thriving in Broome." He slid her a dry look. "I doubt you'd find Vikki critical on that point. She's quite the queen bee in the Chinese community."

Being the keeper of the Picard home probably carried a certain status, Christabel thought, and being of a venerable age undoubtedly carried weight. She wasn't really expecting the bright and shrewd intelligence that came straight at her from the old woman's eyes when she straightened up from talking to Alicia.

Christabel felt herself blushing. Nothing was escaping those eyes. They had her stripped and logged in detail, with probably a character analysis done, as well. It took staunch discipline to keep walking up the steps to the veranda, her spine automatically stiffening at feeling herself scrutinised so comprehensively.

It reminded Christabel of her first meeting with Bernhard Kruger after she'd married his son.

Was she suitable?

Would she fit into the right mould?

Would she deliver what was required of her?

She'd had no conception of what she was getting into then. But she did here, with Jared's world, and no matter what she felt with him, the conviction came very strongly that it was wrong to even touch it as she had.

"Vikki Chan…Christabel Valdez," Jared casually introduced. "And her daughter, Alicia, whose acquaintance you've obviously already made."

The old woman bowed. "An honour to meet you."

Christabel politely inclined her head. "The honour is mine. It is very kind of you to welcome me."

Vikki Chan raised a smiling face. "Your daughter tells me she'd like to eat out here so she can watch the storm. I wondered if you would prefer inside."

"No. This is fine," Christabel quickly assured her, noting that a table on the veranda had already been set and feeling she didn't want to go farther into this house. It was easier, staying outside. Easier to leave.

"As you wish. I hope you will enjoy the evening."

Only one evening, Christabel recited firmly to herself, as she watched the old woman walk back into her domain, Jared's domain.

Behind her, a clap of thunder boomed with deafening force. It sounded like the crack of doom, warning her she should not have come. But it was *only one evening.* If she kept her head, no more would come from it.

Having screwed up the necessary willpower, she turned to face Jared…and the storm.

CHAPTER FOUR

JAGGED streaks of lightning shattered the blackness of the sky, a dramatic force of nature that was awesome, accompanied as it was by the explosion of thunder that rolled on and on. Christabel had never seen such storms in Europe, but she remembered them from her childhood in Brazil, and the flash floods they'd brought, wreaking havoc.

To Alicia, this was like a magic show, and she kept pointing out the highlights, crying excitedly, "Look! Look!" and clapping her hands with glee. "Oh, that was a big one!"

Jared laughed at her, enjoying her delight, while deftly playing the role of host, pouring them drinks, offering around a bowl of mixed nuts and rice crackers. He didn't bother buttoning his shirt, and Christabel found herself disturbingly distracted by the glimpses of bare chest.

When he handed her a glass of white wine and charmingly asked, "Or would you rather have the fruit juice Vikki made for Alicia?" she took the wine rather than be faced with him serving her another drink, standing close to her, making her too physically aware of him.

Finally he sat down at the table, on the opposite side to where she had settled herself, leaving the chair between them for Alicia, who was happy darting between the table where she helped herself to crackers and juice, and the prime watching position at the top of the veranda steps.

The table was set simply with bamboo placemats, chopsticks placed on little wooden holders, as well as conventional cutlery in case she and Alicia were unskilled with chopsticks. However, the serviettes were of good linen and the glassware fine quality, adding a touch of class to the casual mood Jared was obviously intent on establishing.

He lifted his glass, his eyes brushing over her like dark sensual velvet. "It's good to have you here."

She felt her nipples hardening and leant forward defensively, toying with her glass. "You can't really be lonely, Jared."

"There are empty places in my life. Aren't there in yours?"

She shrugged. "I dare say it's impossible to fill all of them, all the time."

"Filling some of them, some of the time, would help, don't you think?"

"Temporary measures?"

"If that's how it has to be. Better than nothing."

"Maybe the empty place would feel even bigger afterwards."

"Who can count on afterwards? I might be dead tomorrow."

"Not likely," she dryly retorted.

He glanced out at the storm, still unleashing thunderbolts. "My father died when his plane was struck by lightning, flying into Broome."

The stark statement came as a shock to Christabel. "I'm sorry. I didn't know."

His gaze swung back, fastening on hers with compelling intensity. "None of us know the day or the hour, Christabel. I believe people should make the most of the time they have, while they still can."

Certainly her husband hadn't expected to die, not before his father. Laurens had been counting on inheriting all the money and all the power, having fulfilled Bernhard's demand that he marry and beget at least one child. Nevertheless, he had more than made the most of the time he had with every woman he fancied and every bit of fast living he could pack in. It was not an attitude Christabel admired. It carried no caring for others.

She wasn't aware that her face had tightened over the bitter memories until Jared asked, "What are you thinking?"

She lowered her lashes, veiling her expression as she answered, "My husband died in an accident, too. It was a speedboat crash. Human error. Not caused by a storm."

She sipped the wine, deliberately discouraging any pursuit of that topic, wishing she hadn't brought it up. It was a mistake to talk about her marriage, except in the vaguest terms. The speedboat accident had been world news. It was a connection to all she wanted to escape from.

"How long ago did this happen?"

Jared's tone was sympathetic, stirring a savage irony. She didn't mourn Laurens. He'd lost his taste for her when she'd turned into an undesirable lump and he'd killed any shred of feeling she'd had for him with his subsequent behaviour.

"I was eight months pregnant with Alicia," she said flatly, careful not to give an actual date.

He seemed to weigh that statement before slowly commenting, "So Alicia never knew her father."

"I don't believe she feels any empty place on that score, Jared," she replied tersely, her chin lifting in defiant challenge.

"You're *all* she needs?" he queried.

"We manage well together."

"And is she all *you* need, Christabel?"

"She's all I've got," she answered quickly, trying to ignore the searing look that burrowed under her skin, finding and knowing the empty places he'd talked about and promising they didn't have to stay empty.

He was here, ready, willing and able to satisfy at least some needs. Tonight, if she gave her consent. And Christabel was once again riven by the strong temptation to do just that, to take what she could while she could. It was what he'd been offering, wasn't it, with his talk of not counting on an afterwards?

This dangerous train of thought was broken by the return of Vikki Chan, wheeling a traymobile onto the veranda, calling Alicia to her chair and switching on a lantern above the table to light the meal she was about to serve. She then proceeded to set out a platter of honey prawns and a bowl of steaming rice.

"I cooked more than enough for the little one," she informed Christabel, "so you and Jared can have some as a first course if you like."

"Thank you. They look very tasty."

The old woman smiled benevolently at them all. "Help yourselves," she invited, and left them to it.

There was no doubting that Vikki Chan was a superb cook. The honey prawns were the best Christabel had ever tasted, and Alicia even forgot the storm as she consumed her share with uninhibited pleasure, picking them up with her fingers, arguing they tasted better that way, and Jared agreeing with her.

Since finger bowls were set on the table, Christabel didn't fuss. Her mind was busily sorting through the impression that Vikki Chan had not been making any judgment of her this time. She hadn't exactly sensed approval coming from the old Chinese woman, yet there had been a definite acceptance of her being with Jared like this and a warm indulgence towards her daughter.

In between feeding herself, Alicia chatted away with Jared, enjoying his good-humoured attention, and Christabel couldn't help thinking he would be a good father, kind and caring, making any child of his feel special and loved.

Laurens would have turned their daughter over to an army of nannies, conveniently forgetting she even existed.

The means to an end…that was all his child had meant to her husband…all his wife had meant to him, too.

Special and loved…the words kept drumming through her mind, evoking a fierce surge of need to have Jared make her feel special, make her feel loved.

He instantly turned his gaze to her, as though he was instinctively attuned to her feelings and he'd caught this one right at its crest. Whatever he saw in her eyes, his suddenly blazed with a heat that scorched any denial of what flowed between them.

Her breasts started to prickle with excitement, and

a sweet, melting sensation spread towards her thighs. Despite the danger signals her body was sending, she could not wrench her gaze from the hot promise of satisfaction in his. She wanted him to prove that promise, to deliver all she craved from him, making reality of the persistent fantasy that he could and would be the one to make her feel what Laurens had never made her feel, not even on their honeymoon.

Yes...

Jared didn't say the word out loud but she felt him saying it, heard it throbbing in her mind, running through her bloodstream, zinging along every nerve in her body, building a wild exultant demand that went beyond sanity or common sense.

From behind her came a sudden swirl of wind, ruffling her hair, feathering her skin, and a clap of thunder directly above them made her heart leap, yet still that look from Jared held her, burning with an elemental force that defied other elements.

Vikki Chan reappeared. Alicia kept the old woman busy with conversation. The table was cleared. Alicia had sticky hands and she was invited to the kitchen to clean them properly. Advice was tossed back as they departed.

"Better close the shutters on the south side, Jared. The rain will come in with that wind."

It all washed over Christabel.

Jared stood up, so tall and handsome and quintessentially male, he was like a magnet, drawing on all her female instincts, forcing the recognition that some things couldn't be stopped. They were as inevitable as the rain, falling now in heavy drops on the tin roof. The wind caught the loose sides of his white shirt, billowing them out. His tanned skin gleamed under the lantern light.

"The shutters," he murmured, but he didn't move and she knew that he, too, was caught in this thrall of compelling attraction, not wanting to break it.

"I'll help you." The words spilled from her lips, unbidden, and her legs pushed up from the chair so that she was standing, matching up to him.

"Come *with* me," he said.

And she did, her heart pumping wildly as they moved into action together, sharing the task, keenly aware of the mutual feelings driving them.

The shutters were held open by metal rods. These had to be unhooked, lowered, and bolts shot home to secure closure. The wind blew fat splattering raindrops at them as they worked down the southern veranda in tandem—six shutters in all—with Jared, faster than she was, helping her with the last one.

He was so close, close enough for her to smell him, touch him, and she couldn't bring herself to step away. Her breathing was fast, shallow, out of control. Jared pulled the shutter down and they were enveloped in darkness, a warm, steamy, intimate darkness—the wind and rain shut out, beating at the house but unable to reach them.

She heard the metallic scrape of the last bolt being pushed into place. Everything was fastened down now, safe, except for all the feelings she'd tried to suppress running rampant, urging that the darkness be used to find out what she wanted to know, ached to know.

She heard Jared's breath whoosh out and knew it carried unbearable, pent-up tension. Then he was turning to face her and every nerve in her body was taut with anticipation, waiting for the first touch, the first proof that it was right for this to happen. It had to be right. It had to be worth breaking all the rules she'd set. It had to be what she'd yearned for in the darkness of other nights, countless other nights that had been filled with endless loneliness.

Take me, she begged in her feverish mind. *Take me....*

And he did, his arm sweeping around her waist and scooping her against him, plastering her against him as his other hand thrust through her hair, entwining tresses around strong, determined fingers. His chest heaved against the soft squash of her breasts. His thighs felt rock-hard. Then his mouth took hers, pleasuring it with a passion that excited her beyond anything she had known.

He aroused and kept stirring explosive sensations, kiss after kiss, feeding a deep, seemingly bottomless hunger that demanded a feast, not just a taste but an intense savouring of every taste there was. It was so absorbingly wonderful, Christabel revelled in every moment of it, consumed by the sheer power of the greed that seized her, the greed to experience everything there was to be felt with this man.

Her hands were in his hair, clinging to his head, urging the intoxicating intimacy to go on and on. Her body exulted in the hard heat of his, and when he grasped her bottom to lift her into fitting closer to him, it felt so right, so good, knowing how excited he was, wanting the ultimate connection with her, yearning for it every bit as much as she was.

"Stay with me tonight."

He breathed the words over her tingling lips, words that throbbed their passionate need past the fuzzed edges of her mind, stirring a momentary confusion at the interruption to the silent flow of more immediate needs.

"Stay…" he repeated with raw urgency. "Alicia can be put to bed here."

Alicia! Where…? Her mind worked sluggishly. Gone with Vikki Chan to clean her hands.

"You want this, too, Christabel."

His hand on her bottom, pressing recognition of how aroused they both were. There could be no denying what was so self-evident. They both knew it. She wished he hadn't spoken, wished they had just gone on to…but there wasn't time now. That was what he meant. Alicia…Vikki Chan bringing the next course of their dinner…How long had she and Jared been locked together like this?

He lifted his head back from hers. "Look at me!"

His eyes were like black coals, glowing at her. He slid his hand from its enmeshment in her hair and gently cupped her cheek. He spoke slowly, softly, using his words like seductive tentacles, winding around her, binding her to him.

"We want each other. There's nothing wrong in that so just let it be, Christabel. Time to ourselves, doing whatever pleases us, being free of everything else, taking the night and making it our night."

Being free…just for one night…

"Say yes, Christabel. Say you'll stay with me."

"Yes," she said, impelled by more than Jared would ever know to snatch this time from the life she had to lead, the life that was forever burdened by her

blindly naive decision to marry Laurens Kruger. "I
want this night with you, Jared."

One stolen night.

What harm could there be in it?

No harm…just pleasure…with the pleasure King.

And he kissed her again to show her how it
would be.

CHAPTER FIVE

WHAT they had started had to be put on hold until later. They were not alone yet, not in any practical sense, but Christabel felt oddly disconnected to being a mother or a guest in the aftermath of losing her long-held guard against the desires Jared King stirred in her.

It seemed strange, sitting at the table again as though nothing momentous had happened, secretly harbouring the excitement that continued to buzz through her body while Vikki Chan wheeled out the traymobile, reloaded with the next course for dinner. Alicia followed her, holding a cone of chocolate chip ice-cream, and she skipped over to Jared to thank him for the special treat.

Christabel couldn't stop looking at Jared, imagining what they might do when they were absolutely alone together. Was *he* still aroused? Impossible to know with him sitting on the opposite side of the table. He had felt…big. She wondered what he would look like with no clothes on, how he would feel to her then. Magnificently male and completely self-assured about his sexuality, she decided, not having to prove anything, just being himself. And letting her be herself.

"That looks superb, Vikki, as usual," he complimented as the old Chinese woman served them portions of steamed fish and braised vegetables and spooned sauce over them.

"Vikki has a Chinese dish with bamboo sticks in it for cooking the fish, Mummy," Alicia informed her importantly. "She showed me lots of special things. This house has got a really big kitchen. Bigger than our whole caravan."

"That's nice," Christabel answered vaguely, watching Alicia's tongue wrapping itself around the generous scoop of ice-cream, catching the melting drops before they dribbled down the cone.

She thought of Jared's tongue, electrifying her lips, invading her mouth, the exciting intimacy it had generated. Would he kiss her breasts like that, licking in a swirl around her nipples...

"And Vikki's got a shell collection, too," Alicia rattled on. "She said she'd show me when she finished cooking."

"That's nice," Christabel heard herself say again before forcing her mind to really register what her daughter was telling her. She turned to Vikki Chan, who was still spooning sauce. "Thank you for giving Alicia your time."

"No problem. It is a joy to see her delight in things. So it should be with a child."

"Yes," Christabel agreed, happy there was no problem with Alicia. She needed to be free of problems tonight, free to revel in the joy of her own body meeting Jared King's...making love...delighting in every pleasure he promised.

"Your mother will be staying longer than your bedtime, Alicia," Jared smoothly announced, smiling at her daughter. "When you've finished looking at

the shell collection, I'm sure Vikki can find a bedroom for you to sleep in.''

"A whole bedroom for me?" Alicia's eyes
rounded at the intriguing idea before a more trouble-
some thought struck. "Where will you be, Mummy?"

"Here," she answered. "Here with Jared," she
added, her heart filling with the bliss of that reality.
Not fantasy tonight. No restless dreaming, either.
She'd have the warm, strong, flesh-and-blood man
she wanted, touching her in every sense there was.

"There is a bed in the same room as my shells,"
Vikki Chan said encouragingly to Alicia. "Perhaps
you would like that one. Shall we see?"

"Yes," she cried eagerly, only too happy to explore more of the house with the old woman.

They went off together, leaving Christabel and
Jared to eat their dinner by themselves.

Jared refilled their glasses with wine. Christabel
stared at the tight little black curls on his chest. She
remembered her hands ploughing through the thick
springy hair on his head as he kissed her. That was
different, not the kind of hair she could twirl around
her finger. She wondered if the curls would feel soft
or wiry.

Jared lifted his glass as he sat down again. "To
being free," he said, uncannily reading her feelings
as he did so often.

"This one night," she answered, more intoxicated
by all she envisaged having with him than any wine
could make her, but as she sipped the fine, oaky
Chardonnay, its taste brought her palate alive and its
bouquet was sharply fragrant, as though all her senses
were heightened.

The fish was superb, moist, tender, flavoursome. She'd never eaten better. The vegetables and the sauce complemented it perfectly. Unskilled with chopsticks, she automatically used the conventional fork supplied, but she watched Jared using the Chinese implements, the deft control of his fingers, the smooth conveying of food to his mouth, so gracefully sure, never dropping anything.

Everything about him gave her pleasure. And it was such exquisite relief not having to put up defences, to say yes instead of no, to simply let nature take its course without any outside interference. She loved all she knew of Jared King. Tonight she would know more. As much as she could. She'd store it all up in a treasure box of memories and keep it forever.

Jared put down his chopsticks and nodded to her almost empty plate. "Good?"

"Great!" she replied with spontaneous exuberance, not having to guard her words, not having to repress anything for the rest of this night.

He smiled contentedly, sitting back with his glass of wine, watching her finish the last few morsels. It made Christabel very conscious of what he might be thinking as she ate. Was he remembering how little she wore under her dress? He had to know now, having felt the unrestricted contours when he'd held her. Was he envisaging her naked?

Her pulse quickened as she set her fork down and picked up her glass, looking at him over the rim of it as she sipped the wine, seeing the dark simmer in his eyes and feeling her stomach curl in anticipation.

"Shall we leave the table and enjoy the freshness

of the rain?'' he said, surging to his feet without waiting for a reply.

The suggestion startled her. "Do you mean…go out in it?'' The thunder and lightning had given way to a torrential onslaught that was still pouring down. They'd be soaked in seconds.

"No. Just to the edge of the veranda.'' His mouth curved into a sensual tease as he stepped away from his chair, heading for hers. "I can't bear having the table between us any longer.''

"Oh!''

Her excitement soared as Jared moved to the back of her chair. He dropped a kiss on the top of her hair, his warm lips grazing over the waves springing from its centre parting. "Bring your glass of wine with you,'' he murmured persuasively.

It was still in her hand and she stood with it, responding unthinkingly, drawn by the compelling, seductive energy of the man behind her. He whipped away her chair, curled an arm around her waist and moved her out of the pool of lantern light, down the veranda to a more shadowed area and over to the broad balustrade between the posts.

The air did smell fresh with the rain, the oppressive heat dispelled and the dust settled. The black sky was still unbroken, no moon, no stars. She could hear the storm-driven waves in the bay below them roaring and hissing. But they were outside things and she was most conscious of Jared, his hand resting on the curve of her waist and hip, his body half behind hers, brushing against it as he reached past her to set his glass of wine down on the flat width of the balustrade.

Then his arms were wrapped around her midriff,

and his cheek was rubbing against her hair, and his mouth was close to her ear, his voice low and husky as he murmured, "You've held me away from you so long, I have to know this is real."

"Yes," she whispered, hearing the echo of her own need.

"I want to breathe in the scent of your hair…feel it, taste it…"

He trailed hot kisses through it, down her neck, and Christabel instinctively arched back, revelling in the sheer sensuality of his desire for her. She felt him move his thighs apart, nestling her more snugly against him, and one of his hands moved to cup the soft swell of her breast, his thumb sweeping over its peak, fanning it into hard prominence.

She closed her eyes, wanting to focus on inner sensations, unable to resist rolling her bottom against him, inciting more awareness, exulting in the thought of exciting him. She wanted him to touch her other breast. It felt as though it was swelling, aching to be held and caressed, but he abandoned the one he held, his arms sliding down, hands spreading over her stomach, pressing an acute recognition of his arousal.

"I need to touch you and it can't wait," he warned, his fingers gliding towards her thighs, gathering up the soft fabric of her dress. "Tell me now if you've changed your mind."

She had no intention of changing her mind. It was wildly urging him on. And it was impossible to make any reply. Her breath caught in her throat as her skirt was lifted and everything inside her stilled, poised in mesmerised waiting for what would come next. Fingertips grazed the bare flesh under her hips, mak-

ing it pulse with quivery excitement. His thumbs
reached up and hooked onto the slim elasticised
waistband of the G-string. It was drawn down so
swiftly, Christabel barely had time to gasp at the boldness of the move before the flimsy garment was dangling around her ankles.

"Step out of it, Christabel."

"Jared…" It was more a choked cry of shock than
protest.

Instantly his arms were around her hips again, on
top of her skirt now, the fabric having naturally fallen
as his hands had slid her underwear down her legs.
The pressure, back into the cradle of his thighs, was
a provocative reminder of her own wanton actions.

"I'll put it in my pocket," he assured her. "Neither
Vikki nor Alicia will see when they come back. No-
one will know you're naked under that dress except
you…and me. And I want to know it, Christabel. I
want to know you won't change your mind when
Alicia comes to say good-night. I want to know the
yes is still yes."

The passion in his voice sizzled through her. "It
will be," she promised.

"You were in two minds earlier this evening. Make
it decisive now. Don't tease, Christabel. Show me."

Tease… A guilty flush raced up her neck. The way
she'd dressed could only be interpreted as teasing,
had she not come this far with him, and what he said
was true—no one else would know…except them.
And there was something deliciously wicked in being
dressed and naked at the same time. Wicked and sexy
and terribly stimulating, knowing she was so accessible to any intimate touch from him.

She stepped out of the G-string.

He swooped, unbelievably…erotically…kissing the hollows behind her knees as he picked up the scrap of material and scrunched it into his shirt pocket. Then feather-light fingertips swirled up the outside of her calves and her thighs as he slowly straightened up, moving back into position behind her. The caress circled inwards, under her dress, and her whole body went into exquisite suspension again, tremulously waiting for him to reach further… wanting him to stroke her *there*.

But the shock of voices coming down the hallway froze that tantalising progress. Jared's hands slid away and he stepped aside, picking up his wineglass and turning his back to the rain, casually propping himself against the balustrade and studying her face as they waited for the approaching intrusion on their privacy. Christabel found her hand clenched tightly around her own wineglass and was amazed she'd kept holding it all this time.

"You are more beautiful to me than any woman I've ever known," Jared murmured. "And I want this night with you more than I've wanted anything in my life."

She shivered at the passionate intensity in his voice, suddenly fearful he would press for more afterwards. "You are special to me, too," she confessed. "But please understand…."

He pressed a light finger to her lips, halting the words she felt constrained to speak.

"You have a child. And a life you won't share with me. You don't have to tell me that, Christabel. You've told me so in a thousand ways."

"I don't want it to be like this, Jared. It just is," she pleaded.

He nodded. "I want you to know I value the gift…more than I can say."

The gift…it was a lovely way of expressing what they were doing, the giving to each other of what they most wanted, the wonder of it, the pleasure, the satisfaction of finally unwrapping what had only been imagined and knowing all it was.

"Mummy…guess what?"

Christabel felt torn as she turned to face the child who could never be Jared's child. Alicia was owned by her inheritance, and not even her mother could keep that from having its effect in the long run. Both their lives were circumscribed by it, and for several moments Christabel railed against that fate, having to remind herself that her daughter was the innocent victim of it before she could rise above a fierce wave of resentment and smile at the child she loved, now circling the table, assisting the old woman who'd accompanied her in clearing it.

"What am I to guess, Alicia?" She set her wineglass down on the balustrade, ready to attend to her daughter's needs.

"You don't have to tell me a story tonight 'cause Vikki said she would. She knows about dragons."

"That sounds exciting."

"And I'm going to sleep in the shell room."

"It's all settled then?"

"Yes," Vikki Chan answered, nodding reassurance as she added, "I'll tuck the little one into bed and see that she sleeps."

"It's very good of you."

"A pleasure."

"And thank you for the delicious meal," Christabel said belatedly, wondering just how much the old woman encompassed in her understanding. Not that it mattered. She would probably never meet Vikki Chan again. One night was one night.

"There's some ice-cream left over if you want it, Mummy."

"No. I've had enough, Alicia." The only food she wanted now was food for the soul, her own private feast of memories that might make some sense of being a woman, not just a mother.

"I'll look after coffee, Vikki," Jared slid in. "Thank you for everything."

The old woman flashed him a wise look as she finished clearing the table. "Then I shall retire, too." Having loaded the last things onto the traymobile, she turned an indulgent smile to Alicia. "You'd best say good-night to your mother now. We have much to do."

"Yes. We have lots to do," came the eager agreement. "Good night, Mummy," she cried, running towards her, arms outflung for a hug and a kiss.

Christabel had an electric few moments, hoping her daughter's feet wouldn't catch the hem of her dress as she scooped her up in their usual embrace. To her intense relief, she managed to negotiate the lift safely, with Alicia perched happily against her shoulder as they exchanged good-night kisses.

"Do I get a good-night kiss, too?" Jared asked teasingly, moving into an easily accessible position beside Christabel.

Alicia giggled and slid over to plant one on his

offered cheek. It was done without the slightest hesitation, and although Jared wasn't a stranger to her daughter, it was unusual for her to be so readily familiar with a man. Was it a natural affinity, an instinctive liking and trusting?

There was no future for them with Jared King, Christabel savagely reminded herself as she lowered Alicia to her feet again. There was no point in wondering about how good he might be for a fatherless child.

"Off you go," she urged Alicia. "I'll come and get you when it's time to leave."

"It's the shell room, Mummy."

"I'll show her where it is," Jared assured her.

"Good night to both of you," Vikki Chan said, bowing benevolently before wheeling the traymobile away, back into the house, Alicia trailing after her, asking about dragons.

There were too many dragons to fight, Christabel thought, suddenly swamped by a wave of wretched misery. Money was a curse, a terrible, terrible curse, and she was powerless to make it go away. Apart from everything else, there was always the question...had the speedboat been sabotaged?

Laurens dead, Bernhard dying of cancer despite the best medical treatment in the world...no-one to question what the money men did with the Kruger fortune once Bernhard was gone. The heir was a child who could be controlled, manipulated...*disposed of if necessary*?

Christabel shivered.

A warm arm encircled her shoulders. "She's safe with Vikki."

Safe? Not even an army of bodyguards could keep them *safe*! And what kind of life was that—imprisoned in a golden cage, never knowing who could be trusted when there was so much money at stake?

Tonight was one little window of freedom.

She sighed away her angst, determined not to let it intrude on her time with Jared. It was too precious to lose, even one second of it.

"So now we're alone," she said, lifting her hands to do what she had wanted to do ever since he'd come to open the gate for her. She slid her fingers through the black curls on his chest and smiled up at him. "I want to touch you, too."

CHAPTER SIX

TIGER eyes smiling at him...

The thought crossed Jared's mind, even as his skin seemed to leap with exultation at the sheer pleasure of her touch. There was more at stake here than fulfilling fantasies, he swiftly told himself. He sensed something deeply primitive working through her, an almost savage intent flowing through the fingers curling through his chest hair, her nails lightly scraping.

She had decided.

Now she was following through.

Was it with the heart of a tiger going for its kill, taking quickly, feasting quickly, walking away with a satisfied appetite?

No!

The fierce protest ripped through Jared.

This night would go *his* way!

One night, she'd said, but one night was never going to be enough for him. He had to make her feel it wasn't enough for her, either.

Her palms slid sensuously up to his shoulders, moving his shirt off them. He had to seize control before she tipped him out of it, make the moves his, not hers, slow everything down. But before he could stop her, she leaned forward and ran her tongue over his nipple, then pressed her mouth around it and...he couldn't bring himself to make any move.

His mind slid into meltdown, fired by her desire

for him and exploding with the sensations she was evoking, tasting him so erotically, and her hands gliding down his arms, pushing the sleeves of his shirt ahead of them. His stomach was contracting, his heart beating like a drum, wanting her mouth to move to that side, too. His shirt was dropping off him. He caught one sleeve as it fell past his hand, not knowing why, only that it was something to catch, to hold on to.

Then her hands were stroking the sensitive flesh under his rib cage and she kissed him over his heart. He had no control over his erection. His body had a life of its own and he felt it straining upwards, wanting her touch, yet he knew it would be over then and there if she did reach down and...fingers sliding under the waistband of his shorts.

He had to stop her.

Now!

He grabbed her under her arms, hauled her up and kissed her, ravishing the mouth that had ravished his body. She came up on tiptoe, flinging her arms over his shoulders, raking his back with her nails, as passionately intense as he in her wanting, kissing him back with a wild fervour that almost took him past the point of no return again.

He carried her to the balustrade, shoved his shirt over the bare wood, sat her on it and lifted his head back to draw breath. Her eyes were glazed amber, her lips still parted. The realisation hit him she had acted instinctively, compulsively, driven by desires she hadn't fully recognised, let alone planned on carrying out.

"Christabel..."

The soft call of her name cleared the glaze from her eyes and she looked at him with such vulnerable appeal his heart turned over. He lifted his hand to her cheek, stroking with a tender caring he hoped she felt.

"I want to love you...not take you."

"Was I doing something wrong?" she asked anxiously.

And he knew then, knew beyond a shadow of a doubt that what she was doing with him was new to her, that her struggle all along was not only with his interest in her, but with a sexual awakening she hadn't known how to cope with, and tonight it had become a stronger force than all the other hidden forces in her life.

What manner of man had she married for her to be so unsure of herself? He shook that enigma out of his mind. The only important thing was she'd never known *this* deep an arousal with any other man. It was as unique to her as it was to him and right now she needed to be reassured.

"No. Nothing wrong. Just too fast. You would have had me coming before I could make it special for you," he gently explained.

"Oh!"

He felt her cheek warm and to nullify any embarrassment he'd stirred, he bent and ran his tongue over the inner tissue of her parted lips. Then he kissed her slowly, sensually, determined on keeping urgency at bay, wanting to show her how it could be for them, making love.

He dropped his hand to her shoulder and gradually stretched the low neckline of her dress, shifting the bodice down below one elbow so he could lift her arm out of it, effectively baring her breast. She moaned as he filled his hand with the soft, yielding fullness of her naked flesh, and to his ears it was the sound of longing.

Sensing he had done what she wanted done to her, he bent and covered the dark areola with his mouth, swirling his tongue around it, lashing the distended nipple, tugging lightly on it with his teeth, exciting himself as her breathing quickened and he gently squeezed her breast in a pumping action. She clutched at his head, urging him on, emitting sexy little cries of intense pleasure.

She wanted more, was begging for more. He dragged the rest of her bodice down, freeing her other breast, and she actually grabbed his head and moved it across, expelling a ragged sigh as he answered the raging desire, working the deep, sensual magic he knew was coursing through her, building the ache, building the need, using his hand to keep the sensations flowing through both her breasts, and when she wrapped her legs around him and arched back, he knew she was teetering on the edge of climax.

He wound his arms around her, scooped her off the balustrade and crushed her to him, loving the naked moistness between her thighs rubbing against his bare stomach as he carried her, his face buried in the deep valley between her breasts, revelling in her lush femininity.

"Jared...what...where?" She was disoriented, confused, hanging onto his head.

"Going to turn off the light above the table," he explained.

"Oh! Was it...was it like that for you when I...when I...?"

"Yes."

"I've never felt like this." She sounded dazed, disbelieving.

"Neither have I."

It was the truth. He was seized with an all-consuming desire to give her everything she'd never known, for him to be the one she would always remember, her first real lover. And the one man she'd want to keep in her life, the one she couldn't resist sharing herself with.

He closed the front door, blocking any sound from carrying through the house, switched off the pool of light thrown by the lantern and spread Christabel across the table.

"What are you doing?" she gasped in bewilderment.

"Freeing my hands so I can finish taking off your dress."

She laughed in surprise, wriggling to help him. "Your shorts, too. I want you as naked as me."

He swiftly removed his remaining clothes, then slid her dress down her legs, ridding her feet of sandals at the same time.

"Touch your breasts, Christabel," he softly advised her as he parted her legs and moved between them, stroking her inner thighs. "Feel them as I felt them. Know them as I did...beautiful, sensual, full of womanly excitement. Do it as I do this...."

Very gently he moved his caressing to her moist lower lips. "Close your eyes. Think only of feeling," he murmured, swooping down to kiss and stroke and tease into intense arousal the most intimate part of her, spreading one hand through the silky hair above it to hold her still for him, sliding the other down the softly swollen folds, deepening the caress, circling the passage inwards, feeling the convulsive clutch of her muscles as he moved his mouth over and around the peak of excitement and breathed in the musky scent of her rush of desire for him...so sweet and heady and intoxicating.

"Jared..."

His name bursting needfully from her throat as she quivered, writhed, and he was filled with a wild exultation...Christabel calling for him...her man...the only one to make her feel like this.

"Jared...please...I can't bear it.... I can't...."

"Yes, you can," he soothed, moving to answer her need. "Go with it. Let it happen."

And he kissed his way up her pulsating body, deftly replacing the caress of his hand with the extension of himself she really craved...the glorious exhilaration of feeling her convulse around him in frantic welcome as he entered, pushing slowly inwards, providing the solidity for her to shatter around.

"Oh..." She arched in ecstasy.

He paused, kissing the highly thrusted peaks of her breasts.

"Oh...oh..." Tremulous waves rolling through her. She suddenly grabbed him, fiercely pulling him upwards. "More...more, Jared."

He gave her the full length of himself, plunging hard and fast to the inner rim of her womb, and again she arched, loving all he could give, and the blissful,

"Oh!" as she felt the completion of his thrust poured a sweet elation through Jared.

He kissed her mouth, passionately reinforcing the intimate link of their bodies. Her arms wrapped around him. Her legs wrapped around him. She clung to him, greedy for every sensation of this deep and mutual possession of each other, hugging him so tightly, he knew she wanted the feeling prolonged forever.

"Jared, this is so incredibly wonderful," she breathed against his lips.

The joy of her uninhibited heart zinged through his heart, instantly compelling the urge to control his own need while giving her all the pleasure he could. "It will keep coming," he promised. "Just ride with it now."

One orgasm—even if it was her first—wasn't special enough. Wanting her to feel a rolling sequence of them, Jared moved them both into alternating rhythms—fast and slow—reading her response, her need, driving her to each quivering pinnacle, riding the crest of it, sliding to the next one, loving the voluptuous roll of her body as she flowed with him and around him, the little cries of pleasure that burst from her throat, the sheer abandonment of herself to him.

His excitement in giving her this pleasure became so intense, he could not contain it any longer, and the last shred of control left him as he drove towards answering his own urgent need. She was so hot, so welcoming, so deliciously open to him, it was impossible to slow the compelling rush towards climax. Tension gripped his body, stretching it to the inevitable burst of sweet violent spasms, and again she wrapped herself around him, revelling in the gift of himself, and she was kissing him, caressing him, loving him, and for Jared it was the most perfect moment of his life.

"You truly are the pleasure King," she murmured in husky wonderment, still pressing soft little kisses on his face. "You truly are."

The title bemused him. "Is that how you think of me?"

"It's in your eyes, the way you touch...even that very first night you came to the markets, you took pleasure in running your fingers over my jewellery display, and when you looked at me..." She sighed, her warm breath feathering his cheek.

"Looking at you gave me pleasure, Christabel, and I want more of it now, looking at you lying on my bed where I've wanted you a thousand times. And that's where I'm taking you right this minute."

She gave a gurgle of delighted laughter as he scooped her up and held her cradled across his chest, his legs purposefully striding down the veranda to the French doors that led into his bedroom. It was coming out right, he thought triumphantly. Christabel hung her arms around his neck and nestled her head on his shoulder, wanting what he wanted.

"The rain has stopped," she observed in surprise.

"So it has," he agreed carelessly.

"A storm to remember," she murmured.

He smiled, interpreting her words as proof of the feelings he'd successfully implanted in her memory.

Once inside his bedroom, he laid her down on the pillows and switched on a table lamp, driven to match the reality of her to the fantasy he'd built up in his mind. He walked around the bed to the other side, feasting his eyes on the sheer perfection of her.

Her glorious hair was just as he'd imagined, a lustrous fan of silky waves, rippling out in sensual invitation, and her skin did gleam like smooth honey. Her body was the very epitome of femininity, lush curves and long, elegant legs, but he saw not a trace of the tiger image he'd imbued her with.

There was almost an awkward self-consciousness in the way she lay there, waiting for him to join her, not shy, but acutely aware of her nakedness and his appraisal of it. Her fingers made agitated little movements, as though uncertain of whether they should cover something, at least a little.

It made him wonder why…how she could not know the power of her sexual attraction…what had undermined the pride and confidence she should have?

Her eyes were not inviting dangerous play. Her eyes were fixed on him, avidly drinking in every detail of his physique as though it was a source of intense inner marvelling. It hit Jared forcefully that everything about this situation was new to her, being with him like this, both of them freely naked, totally unrestricted intimacy with no fear of criticism.

It was oddly moving that she was delighting in him so much, like a child being showered with gifts at a surprise party. He stretched out beside her, propping himself up on his elbow so he could watch the expressions on her face. She smiled at him, no exotic mystery in her eyes, more a twinkle of happy mischief.

"Am I allowed to touch you now?" she asked.

He grinned an open invitation. "All embargoes on touch removed. Go right ahead."

"Anywhere?"

"Whatever takes your fancy."

She immediately sat up in a commanding position, her face wickedly gleeful as she challenged him. "Then you lie down, Jared. Just you lie there and let me do what I want."

"Am I allowed to touch?" he asked teasingly as he settled his head on a pillow, assuming a totally relaxed position.

She cocked her head on one side, considering the question. "No. Better not. You'll distract me and take over and this is my turn."

He was amused and intrigued by what *her turn* would entail.

It very quickly became the most incredibly erotic experience of his life. She touched him as though she was sensually absorbing all that he was—his arms, his body, his legs, every part of him—her soft, beguiling fingerpads making their own paths and patterns, emitting a tingling magic, creating a sensational artistry focused entirely on him.

Wherever she kissed him it was with a kind of fascinated concentration on his response, wanting to know what excited, what pleasured, and clearly delighting in arousing him again. She knelt between his legs, lightly running her nails up and down the taut muscles of his thighs, watching the effect on him, the stiffening swell growing to full hardness. She reached out and wrapped her fingers around him, then gently cupped him with her other hand, squeezing as she bent over and took him in her mouth, rhythmically inciting the most intense and exquisite pleasure.

Her hair was spread all around him—his stomach, groin, thighs—silkily feathering his highly sensitised flesh as she deepened and accelerated the flow of excitement. Apart from the exquisite stimulation she was imparting, the visual pleasure of her was enthralling, lifting the whole experience to levels of intensity that blew Jared's mind. He heard himself calling her name in a wild crescendo of need.

Instantly she lifted herself and moved into straddling him. Then she was taking him inside her, lowering herself slowly, feeling and making him feel the long slide into blissful chaos as he climaxed in a series of violent tremors. Her beautiful breasts brushed his chest as she leaned over, and the soft curtain of her hair enveloped them as she loved his mouth with long, avid kisses.

Jared lost all track of the questions he'd wanted answered about Christabel. For the rest of the night they wallowed in a feast of sensuality, moving around each other, exploring and discovering, indulging an ever-increasing appetite for every possible intimacy, entranced by their connections, stimulated by their almost constant capacity for arousal, their desire to *feel* all that could be felt between them.

They didn't talk. Speech seemed irrelevant. There was a deeper, more elemental communion happening between them, a bonding that was more satisfying, more fulfilling than words could possibly express. This was Jared's instinctive belief, and his instincts had not been wrong about Christabel. She *was* the woman for him, just as certainly as he was the man for her.

When languor finally overtook them, energy completely spent, Jared drifted into sleep, never doubting that the woman he held in his arms would still be there when he stirred again. It didn't occur to him that when the night ended, Christabel would leave him. What she had stipulated earlier was forgotten, overlaid by a sense of unbreakable togetherness.

He simply didn't comprehend—couldn't comprehend—had no way of even beginning to comprehend—that for her, it had to remain...

Only one night.

CHAPTER SEVEN

SOMETHING felt wrong.

Jared was barely conscious, swimming out of deep sleep, yet he was instinctively reaching out, expecting, wanting and...there was only empty space!

It jolted him awake. Daylight hit his eyes. He was alone in his bed. Had Christabel gone to check on her daughter? How late in the morning was it?

His gaze darted to the clock radio on the bedside table, already thinking it was set to switch on at seven o'clock. It showed twelve minutes short of that. Still early, but the child was probably awake. Christabel would be very conscious of Alicia waking in a strange house, probably wanting to find her mother. Maybe she had come looking.

Jared frowned at that thought, then dismissed it. Like most old people, Vikki Chan slept lightly. She would have heard Alicia stirring, would have reassured the child, looked after her. It had to be Christabel's strong protective instincts making her act.

He rolled out of bed, wanting to be with her, wanting to forge a good relationship with her daughter, as well. He was striding towards his en suite bathroom for a quick shower and shave when the thought struck him—Christabel would not have gone to her daughter naked. They'd left their clothes on the veranda. Had she retrieved them?

76

He turned towards the French doors, then paused, noticing his white shorts and shirt draped over the armrest of the chair nearest the doors. Christabel had tidied up. He walked over to the chair and checked his shirt pocket looking for the G-string he'd tucked into it last night. The pocket was empty. As empty as his bed.

An unease slid into his mind...an unease he couldn't shake. He strode to his wardrobe, took out a *yukata*, quickly wrapped himself in the handy cotton robe, and with his heart hammering, took the swiftest route through the house to the shell room.

No Christabel.

No Alicia.

He made straight for the kitchen. Vikki Chan was measuring coffee grounds into the percolator. "When did they leave?" he asked, not bothering with any preamble. The need to know was too urgent, too vitally important.

"At first light," she answered, looking at him with eyes that understood his frustration.

"Did you speak to her?"

"No. I'd left the door to the shell room open so I could hear the child if she woke. She didn't wake. Her mother came and took her at first light. I heard the Cherokee she drives start up and leave."

Jared expelled a long hissing breath through his teeth.

"It was not my place to stop her, Jared."

He shook his head, stating the bleak truth, "She would not have been stopped anyway."

The night was over at dawn. That was when she'd

left him. First light. Nothing had changed for her. Nothing!

"It's Monday, Jared. A school day for the child," Vikki reminded him.

"If that was all Christabel had on her mind, she would have told me."

Vikki nodded, not arguing the case, accepting he knew better. "She carries many burdens, that one. She does not know what freedom is."

She did last night. For a little while. The need to hold onto that had Jared clenching his hands.

"You cannot fight her sense of responsibility, Jared," Vikki quietly advised. "You must lift it from her shoulders if you are to win."

"I don't know what *it* is! If I did…"

"She did not talk?"

"Not of that. In all the time I've known her…"

"She remains one step removed," Vikki finished for him. "Yes, I saw that last night. I was wrong about her playing woman games with you. She wants you but…"

"But what?" Jared pushed as she paused, frowning.

She shrugged. "It is for you to find out. All I know is this. The goodness in the child comes from the mother. There is a strong wall of integrity in Christabel Valdez which will not be broken. I think she does, and will always do, what she believes is right."

It was *right* for them to be together. How could she turn her back on what they had shared last night? How could she let it go?

Maybe she hadn't. It *was* a school day. And she

was supposed to come in to the office this morning. He'd arranged the meeting with her before going to Hong Kong, ostensibly to show her photographs of the special jewellery display—her designs for the Picard pearls—and hopefully discuss a further set of designs, a career with him.

She'd vetoed any idea of a career yesterday afternoon but there were still the photographs. He hadn't brought them out last night. If Christabel was still planning to see him at work once Alicia was off at school…he could be misinterpreting her departure at first light.

He gave himself a mental shake. Last night had meant so much to him, it had been a shock finding Christabel gone. Nevertheless, there was no need to go overboard on that action as yet. Vikki Chan was a shrewd judge of character. Christabel would do what she believed was right, bypassing any fuss over taking Alicia home, keeping the child uninvolved in their relationship until more was sorted out between them.

"I'm blowing this out of proportion," he muttered.

Vikki raised her eyebrows queryingly.

He gave her an ironic smile. "You're right. It is a school day. And a workday for me."

"Breakfast as usual?"

"Yes. Thank you." He turned to go, heading for the bathroom again.

"Your mother comes back today," Vikki called after him.

"So she does," he tossed back without pausing.

He didn't care what his mother knew about Christabel. She and Vikki could speculate all they liked about the relationship. He knew his mother would keep her own counsel unless he asked for it and he had no intention of asking for it.

Vikki hadn't told him anything he hadn't known. His mother had no better information. The only person who could tell him what he needed to know was Christabel herself, and it was well past time she started talking to him about the burdens she carried.

The long shadow cast by her dead husband.

Her fear of a man in a suit.

Had either of those burdens been diminished during their long night of loving?

Surely she would be more ready to be open with him when they met this morning. He had won her trust last night. More than her trust. They had made love for hours. It had to mean more to her than one night of sex with him.

The eleven o'clock appointment time they had agreed upon came and went. The photographs were spread across his desk, ready for Christabel to see, but the minutes kept ticking past as Jared waited and waited for her to arrive, his inner tension rising with the return of his earlier thoughts.

He remembered his toast to being free.

This one night, she'd answered.

One night.

He'd been so sure he could make it more.

Somehow he had to make it more.

A knock on his office door brought a leap of hope. She'd come. A bit late but…

His mother entered.

Jared slumped back in his chair, disappointment knifing through him.

"How was the trip?" she asked.

He summoned the energy to announce an enthusiastic, "Great!" then recollected she had spent the weekend with the Connelly family, planning the wedding between Samantha Connelly and his brother Tommy—true love having finally won out for those two. A stab of envy hit him as he asked, "Got the wedding on track?"

"They've settled on having it at Kununurra." She walked over to his desk. "Photographs of Christabel's designs?"

"Yes. They were a big hit with the Hong Kong traders."

She perused the shots he'd taken of the display. "They do look splendid. You were right about her talent, Jared." Her gaze swept up, the sharp intelligence in her dark eyes nailing him. "Will she do more for us?"

He smiled with ironic whimsy. "Who can tell with Christabel?"

"She's your enterprise, Jared."

He shrugged. "I had intended negotiating a new deal with her this morning. She hasn't shown...yet."

"And if she doesn't?"

"I don't have the right to order her time. You know that. The choice is hers."

"Nothing has changed?"

He knew it was an oblique reference to last night. She would have been to the house after the flight back to Broome, probably changed clothes before coming on here. Vikki would not have held anything back from his mother.

"Not in that respect, no," he answered, denying her any more personal insight.

Her gaze wavered. The corner of her mouth almost turned down into a grimace but she checked it. Jared sensed her vexation. She didn't like the situation with Christabel Valdez. There were too many unknowns for her to feel comfortable with it. Jared well understood her feeling, but it wasn't going to stop him. Some things couldn't be stopped.

She affected a dismissive little smile. "Well, I just dropped in to say hello. I must go and check my mail. We'll discuss the Hong Kong business after lunch."

"Fine," Jared agreed.

A tactful retreat…in case Christabel did come this morning…although it was now eleven-forty and looking highly unlikely.

He watched his mother leave. She always moved with dignity and grace. Everyone in the Kimberly referred to her as a great lady—Elizabeth Picard King of Broome and King's Eden. She was sixty-two but the only giveaway to that age was her white hair, which looked quite stunning framing a relatively unlined face—still a very striking face, dominated by her eyes and the strength of character that always shone through.

He loved and admired his mother. His father may have been the major influence in his two older brothers' lives, certainly Nathan's—the oldest son—and perhaps Tommy's, as well. Lachlan King had been a legend in his time, as had the King men before him, running the great cattle station of King's Eden.

Jared had loved and respected his father but he'd never wanted to walk in his shoes or take on his territory. Whether it was because he was the youngest son of three, or because he'd been more drawn to the Picard family's pearl industry, he'd always felt closer to his mother than he had to his father. His mother was a very special person, the most special in his life before Christabel.

Now…he had to find the answers that would make sense of Christabel's decisions. He couldn't force them from her. What he needed was more time together. She had denied him that this morning. Perhaps the strength of feeling between them last night had frightened her off. She might think he'd feel justified in making demands, putting pressure on the independent stance she insisted on maintaining.

Jared was quite certain that would not be a winning move. If she was feeling vulnerable, better to let her make the next move when she wanted to. She had to *want* to be with him, Jared reasoned. As much as he wanted to be with her. So it was a matter of leaving the door open for her to enter when she chose.

At twelve noon he picked up the telephone and dialled the number for the Town Beach Caravan Park. As expected, the call was answered by the manager, Brian Galloway, an old-time Broome personality. He was a big man with a big booming voice and a big beer belly, generally liked by everyone.

"Brian, it's Jared King here."

"And what can I be doing for you?" came the jovial response.

"I was expecting Christabel Valdez here at Picard headquarters this morning. She hasn't kept her appointment. Could I leave a message with you for her to call me at her convenience, set up another business meeting?''

"Sure thing. Leave it to me. I'll make sure the little lady gets the message.''

"Thank you, Brian. It is important.''

"No problem. Do it as soon as I can.''

"I'm much obliged.''

She had shown interest in the photographs yesterday. She would surely want her curiosity about the display of her designs satisfied. A business meeting could not be threatening to her. She had always kept control over what she did for Picard pearls. If she was feeling nervous, apprehensive over what he might have assumed from last night, this assurance of strictly business should give her enough confidence to walk through his door again.

Then what?

Grab her and make love on the desk? Make her feel so much that she'd spill out *why* they couldn't be together? His hands clenched into hard fists. He had to get hold of something he could fight, and fight he would to his dying breath. Christabel was his woman, and after last night, he had every right to fight for her. If only she'd let him!

The surge of fierce aggression gradually ebbed and he settled back into accepting the mental challenge she'd always posed. Giving her time and space had worked before. He'd give it a chance to work again before going after her. But the urge to confront was so strong, it was going to be hell holding a patient line, now that he knew what they could have together.

So how long would he give her?

Until he couldn't stand it any longer.

No call came that afternoon.

No call came on Tuesday.

By the end of the second day, Jared could not contain his frustration at Christabel's silence. They did have a business arrangement. The courtesy of a call didn't cost much.

If she'd got his message.

He snatched up the telephone and called Brian Galloway again.

"Jared King here, Brian. Were you able to get my message to Christabel Valdez?" he asked, schooling his voice to a tone of pleasant inquiry.

"Yep. Gave it to her yesterday when she came back with her daughter after school."

"Ah…thank you."

"She's been out all day today, as well. Might not have been convenient to call you. But she's home now. Do you want me to give her a reminder?"

"No…no…that's fine. Just wanted to be sure she got the message. Thanks, Brian."

She was home now, he thought, as he put the telephone down, itching to drive straight over to Town Beach and…but what could be said—or done—in front of Alicia? Bad move. He had to wait for Christabel to come to him. Time alone together. That was what he needed for progress to be made.

Besides, the fact she'd been out both days until Alicia came home from school meant she'd been deliberately avoiding any personal visit from him. Maybe she needed time to think, to reappraise the situation. He could only hope she was moving towards positive decisions, not negative ones.

Wednesday...

He'd been at his office desk for an hour when he remembered Alicia chatting to him about a special school excursion to the bird observatory. He was almost sure she'd said Wednesday. Which probably meant Christabel would have accompanied the class group. Mothers were called upon to help supervise such outings.

He'd been pushing paper around his desk, keyed up for a call that wasn't about to come. Deciding on some physical activity, he got up and went to his mother's office, poking his head around her door to announce, "I'm going out to the pearl farm, see how the shell fishing is progressing. I'll be back after lunch."

She simply nodded, aware of his disinclination to talk.

Half an hour later he was on the Beagle Bay Road out of Broome, hoping for a day of distraction. He was no longer expecting any calls. When his car phone beeped, he frowned at it before leaning forward and activating the receiver. It wouldn't be Christabel. She didn't have this number.

"Jared King," he said, automatically identifying himself.

"Jared..." His mother's voice. "...I have some gentlemen in my office inquiring about Christabel Valdez."

Every nerve in his body leapt to red alert. He put his foot on the brake, slowing the four-wheel drive to a halt while his mind zipped through possibilities.

"Men in suits?" he asked.

"Yes."

"Where are they from?"

"I've been given to understand that Mr. Santiso, Mr. Vogel and Mr. Wissmann have flown all the way from Europe to talk to Christabel. At the moment they are trying to locate her. Brian Galloway of the Town Beach Caravan Park informed them of her connection with Picard Pearls and mentioned that she might have contacted you today."

Big guns from Europe. The formality in his mother's voice meant she was dealing with power. The long shadow of Christabel's dead husband?

"Yes, she did," Jared lied. "In fact, I'll be meeting her in about an hour's time."

Long before the men in suits got to her!

"At the pearl farm?" his mother smoothly inquired, knowing there was no way they could reach her before he did, even if he was speaking the truth.

"Yes. I would expect Christabel to be back in Broome in time to pick her daughter up from school this afternoon. However, if they want to pass on a message…?"

He heard his mother offer what he'd fed to her and snatches of the ensuing conversation. Finally, "No message, Jared. Thank you for your information."

They didn't need to leave a message, Jared reasoned. They thought they had Alicia as hostage to Christabel's return to Broome.

Santiso, Vogel, Wissmann…he recited their names, memorising them as he turned the four-wheel drive around and headed back to Broome as fast as he safely could. The bird observatory was eighteen kil-

ometres on the other side of the township. He prayed
Christabel was there with her daughter.

This was crunch time.

He knew it in his bones.

Christabel was frightened of men in suits.

She had to choose him.

CHAPTER EIGHT

IT WAS quite incredible, the huge flocks of waders at Crab Creek, Christabel thought, listening to the teacher identify the bird species for the children, though missing the names herself. Focusing her attention on anything external seemed beyond her. The constant mental and emotional turmoil over Jared King could not be pushed aside, and each day brought more urgency to the decision she had to face.

Stay or go…stay or go…stay or go…

It was like water torture on her brain, and her heart was so screwed up from wanting more of him, it literally ached all the time. She couldn't keep Jared dangling as she had since Sunday night. One way or another, she had to decide and act on the decision. After what they'd shared together, he had to be feeling as deeply affected as she was, and it simply wasn't fair to keep avoiding a meeting with him or even holding him at a distance as she had before.

She didn't regret her night with him. Never would, she thought fiercely. It had been the best night of her life, and she could live off the memories of it for a long, long time. Yet…it made it so hard to walk away from. She didn't want to live off memories. She desperately wanted what they'd shared to keep on going, to follow its natural course to…

Was it tempting too many fates to remain here, to fully embrace the simplicity of just being a woman in love with Jared King? Was it possible that she and Alicia could live out normal lives, untainted by an inheritance that distorted everything? If she was careful...*they* hadn't tracked her to this outback haven so far. Could she take the chance they never would?

Her whole being yearned for more time with Jared, a continuance of the intimacy he'd led her into. It had felt as though they were truly soul mates on a level nothing else could touch. If they could just journey on together, maybe the answers to her situation would somehow become clearer and the burden she carried could be moved aside to a place of less and less importance.

A flurry of beating wings drew her attention to a flock taking off behind her...birds flying free. Was it a good omen, she thought fancifully, turning to watch them. Her heart leapt into a wild flutter as she caught sight of what had disturbed them into flight...the man striding fast and purposefully towards the class group...the man she'd last seen naked...the man who had just as powerful an impact fully dressed...Jared King.

He wasn't waiting for her decision.

He'd come to claim her as his woman.

She knew it, knew it with intuitive certainty, and she stood mesmerised, feeling her stomach contract in remembered excitement. Her mind jolted through fear of the consequences and surges of dizzying pleasure. He shouldn't be here but he was...he was...he was...and even from the short distance left between them he emitted an energy that swirled around her and held her captive. She couldn't tear her eyes off him.

He wore business clothes—sports shirt, tailored shorts, long socks, lace-up shoes—not dressed for a birdwatching stroll. He'd come from work, and the grimly determined set of his face telegraphed that he would not be turned away. Not by anything. And a sense of panic started welling inside her, diffusing the pleasure of his presence. She'd stolen one night with him. Could she really keep stealing more and more time without bringing a terrible punishment on both of them?

"Christabel..."

He spoke her name in a commanding tone, just as he waved her aside from the group in a commanding gesture. The urgent intensity in his dark eyes drew her into obeying, even as her mind frantically warned of the dangers inherent in involving herself further in this relationship. She tried to gather her defences as she stepped over to where he'd halted, out of ready earshot of the children, but there was no defence that could have withstood the shock of his next words.

"What do the names Santiso, Vogel and Wissmann mean to you?"

Her heart stopped. The safety net she thought she had instantly disintegrated. They'd come. She'd stayed too long and they'd caught up with her.

"Alicia..." The name tripped off her tongue in alarm as she instinctively swung to check where her daughter was.

A hand fell on her shoulder, gripping, halting any further movement. "She's right there with her teacher," Jared assured her. "None of the men I named know where you are. They think Alicia is at school and you're at the pearl farm with me. I bought you time if time is what you want."

She looked at him, dazed by his understanding. "Where are they?" she asked, struggling to contain the full-blown panic the knowledge of their arrival had triggered.

"Last I heard they were in my mother's office at Picard headquarters. I was on my way to the pearl farm when she called me. I said you were meeting me there."

"Why did you put yourself between me and them?" she cried, anguished by his personal interference. It was the last thing she'd wanted, Jared drawing the attention of men like Rafael Santiso to him. It was what had stopped her from...too late now. Wretchedly she sought to explain the situation. "You don't know..."

"I know you're afraid of them," he cut in forcefully. "You've been running from them, Christabel. I don't know how long you've been on the run but that's why you're here, isn't it? The Australian outback seemed safe."

"There's nowhere safe," she muttered bitterly. It was over—her chance with Jared. Over before it had barely begun.

"Yes, there is."

His insistence was hollow to her, words that had no substance in the sickening reality she knew only too well. She shook her head despairingly. "They'll be more watchful this time. I won't get the chance to give them the slip again."

"We do it now. Go and collect Alicia and tell the teacher that both of you are leaving with me."

The aggressive assertiveness in his voice rattled her. "I can't let you get involved," she cried. "It's bad enough that..."

"I am involved, Christabel," he retorted vehemently.

"You don't need to be," she argued just as vehemently. "You can say I didn't turn up at the pearl farm. I won't drag you into this, Jared."

"I won't walk away. Not when you're in trouble and I can give you a way out." His eyes burned into hers with steady resolution as he reasoned, "You came here in the excursion bus. They'll have you if you go back to Broome in it. I can take you to a safe place. It will give you time to plan what you want to do."

Time...her whirling mind seized on the sliver of hope he was offering. Everything within her recoiled from going back to *them* and the dreadful life they would impose on her and Alicia. Jared had bought her time with his interference and maybe she could make good use of it. Any postponement of the inevitable was better than giving up.

"Where can we go?" she fretted. "The road only leads here and back to Broome."

"The airport." He took a mobile telephone out of his shirt pocket. "I'll ring KingAir now to get a plane ready to fly."

KingAir...the charter company owned by his brother Tommy. Of course! She and Alicia could fly anywhere. And hopefully Jared's part in their escape could be covered up. A charter service was in the public domain. Just because his brother owned it didn't necessarily mean her use of it was tied to the King family in any personal sense.

"I can pay for it. One thing I'm not short of is money," she said with savage irony.

"Fine! Get Alicia and we'll leave now."

She left him talking to someone in the KingAir office on his mobile, confident he could charter a plane for them at a moment's notice. Christabel didn't doubt he would manage it, one way or another. He was so positive about getting her and Alicia to a safe place, she let herself hope it could really happen.

As she approached the class teacher, her mind was already racing over a course of action. The emergency funds hidden behind the lining of her handbag would take her anywhere she decided to go, buy anything she and Alicia required until such time as she could get back to the safety deposit box in Sydney. The caravan and the Cherokee could be left behind. Best to completely abandon them.

The teacher was sympathetic to her apologies for leaving the group, accepting the explanation that she had to take Alicia to meet some people who'd arrived unexpectedly in Broome. Which neatly covered Jared's coming to collect her.

Alicia, of course, had more awkward questions for her to handle. "Why can't we stay, Mummy?" she half-wailed as Christabel took her hand and drew her away from her friends.

"Because we have to leave."

"But we were going to have a picnic on the beach."

"Jared is taking us somewhere better."

"Where?" she demanded truculently.

"It's a surprise."

"I don't want a surprise. I like it here."

"Don't argue with me, Alicia. We're going with Jared and that's that."

She huffed and sulked.

"Don't shame me with bad behaviour in front of Jared," Christabel tersely reproved. "He's been very kind to us."

Another more resigned sigh, then a spark of interest. "Are we going to his house again?"

"We'll have to wait and see."

Jared was replacing his mobile telephone in his pocket as they joined him. He gave Christabel a nod of confirmation, then smiled at Alicia, projecting his usual charming manner.

"Sorry to take you away from your friends, but I do have a special treat lined up for you."

She instantly brightened, her little face lighting with eager curiosity. "What is it?"

"Well..." He took her other hand, intent on hurrying the three of them along as they set off together. "...instead of watching birds, I thought you might like to zoom off into the sky like one."

"You mean in a plane?" she cried excitedly.

"Yes. A small plane. It will give you a bird's view of everything you fly over."

While Jared chatted on with Alicia, explaining how differently places looked from the sky, Christabel forced her mind off the all too distracting rapport that flowed so easily—so *appealingly*—between Jared and her daughter and concentrated on mulling over possible destinations.

Perth or Darwin were big enough cities to hide

them for a while but they'd be the first places Rafael Santiso would target, and since he'd come this far to get them under his thumb again, he'd stop at nothing in searching them out. Alice Springs was a less likely place for him to look, right in the centre of Australia.

She recollected there was a famous train—the Ghan—that ran from there to the city of Adelaide in South Australia. One didn't need identification to buy tickets for a train trip. It might throw off any investigators from picking up her track.

Having made the decision, her thoughts circled around Rafael Santiso, the formidable Argentinian who had once headed the South American branch of the Kruger network. He'd moved very fast to clinch a much higher position after Laurens's death, manoeuvring his way around the other factions to win Bernhard's trust and support, taking the reins of power the moment the old man had passed on. Christabel had never trusted him. He was the one who had benefited most from her husband's fatal *accident*.

Worriedly she glanced at Jared. He didn't realise what he was dealing with. It was a dangerous game, helping her like this, frustrating very powerful interests. Her heart was deeply torn by having to leave him, having to cut him out of her life—this beautiful, wonderful man who'd shown her how it could be when everything felt right and nothing bad intruded— yet it could never be right for them again now.

Any more stolen time with him could put all he held dear in jeopardy. No matter how strong he was, the Kruger juggernaut would run over him, uncaring what was destroyed in serving its best interests.

Somehow she had to figure out a way to keep Jared safely removed from her situation.

By the time they reached the car park and were settled in his big Range Rover, Christabel was ready to lay out her plan. With Alicia in the back seat, she had Jared more or less to herself, seated next to him at the front of the vehicle. Once he'd switched on the engine and set off towards Broome, she broached the subject of avoiding any trouble from his connection to her escape.

"The lie you told your mother about our meeting at the pearl farm...how do you intend to explain that away, Jared?"

He slanted her a wryly amused look. "I don't have to explain it, Christabel."

"You once said to me some things can't be stopped. You can count Santiso as one of those things," she warned.

His face turned grim. "Tell me why you fear him so much."

She ignored his demand for information, rushing out a scenario he could use. "You could say I called you after your mother's call and cancelled our meeting at the pearl farm, explaining about the excursion. Say I cut off the connection too quickly for you to tell me about...about the people asking for me, so you came to the bird observatory to let me know and offer us a lift back to town. I think that's a reasonable story."

"I don't need a story," he said with a hint of exasperation and a look that derided her attempt to clear his involvement with her. "What I need is the truth about these men and what part they play in your life."

"That isn't important," she shot at him anxiously. "What is important is to keep you out of it."

"Out of what, Christabel?" he persisted.

She shook her head. "Please listen to me, Jared. It's for your own good, believe me. Once we get to Broome, you can drop me and Alicia where I parked the Cherokee, near the school. I'll drive to the airport and fix things up with the KingAir office. That way you won't be personally connected to my...my get-away."

He frowned at her. "You're frightened for *me*?"

She closed her eyes at his incredulous tone. "Please...just do as I ask, Jared," she begged flatly.

He made no reply for an agonising length of time. For Christabel, the tension of waiting was so painful she could barely contain the emotions churning through her. She fiercely willed him to agree, to cut himself free of her and Alicia.

"Give me your car keys," he brusquely commanded.

Her eyes flew open in disbelief. "What?"

"Your car keys," he repeated. "I'll see that your Cherokee is parked outside the KingAir office after you're on the plane. That will cover your story, if a story eases your mind."

"But..."

"It will ease my mind to personally see you and Alicia onto a plane and know you're beyond the grasp of the men you fear." He sliced her a look of steely determination. "I'm not letting you out of this vehicle until we arrive at the airport, so just do as I say and give me your car keys."

She had to concede that his plan eliminated any

risk of running across the men she wanted to avoid. Relieved that he seemed to be accepting her cover story, she dug into her handbag for her key ring.

"Make sure it's left in the ignition," she instructed, as she handed over the set of keys she carried.

"I only need the one for the car."

"I'll never use the others again so they don't matter. I won't be coming back, Jared."

"You're prepared to leave everything behind?"

"Yes."

"Including me?"

His eyes seemed to burn into her soul. It hurt so much, more than he'd ever know, to turn her back on what they might have had together. For several moments she couldn't override the yearning that ripped through her. She wanted to reach out and hold onto him, to take whatever he'd offer her, to wallow in his caring, to lean on his strength, to tell him no-one— *no-one*—had given her what he had and she wished they could stay together.

Tears pricked her eyes. She wrenched her gaze away, took a deep breath and forced out the only answer she could give, if she was not to ruin his life in ways he wouldn't comprehend until they hit him. He would end up cursing her for involving him if she didn't finish it now.

"There is no future for us," she stated categorically. "There never was. You asked for one night. It's gone. But I'll always remember it. And I thank you for the memory."

That said it all. Pointless to expand on it even if her throat wasn't choked up. Expressing her feelings might only goad him to insist on standing by her side and she couldn't let him. If she sounded cold and heartless, so much the better. Easier for him to let her go, believing she didn't care enough to hold on.

She kept herself rigidly still, staring ahead, closing him out of her personal space, mentally sealing every crack in her composure, determined not to leave him any opening for a different ending to this final encounter. Jared King was a good man. She might not leave him feeling good about the rather curt end to their relationship, but at least she could ensure nothing worse happened to him because of her.

It should have been a relief to reach the outskirts of Broome, knowing their time together was mercifully short now. Perversely, that reality increased the painful anticipation of parting. Forever, Christabel thought, on a wave of intense misery. In a few more minutes, Jared King would only be a memory for her, and she had a terrible urge to feast her eyes on him while she still could, to stamp every detail of him on her brain. She didn't have a photograph of him. All she would have was a memory and it had to last forever.

But if she looked at him he'd see…he'd feel what she was feeling. Jared was so perceptive, so sensitive to mood changes. She couldn't risk looking. Her hands clenched in savage resistance to the urge that would undermine the attitude she had struck. For his sake, she reminded herself. For his sake she had to be content with the memory of their one night together.

The Range Rover turned onto the road to the airport. She shot a quick glance at Alicia in the back seat, realising she'd been completely quiet on the trip.

Her head was slumped in sleep. She'd nodded off, tired from the long walk at the bird observatory. A five-year-old child, Christabel thought, worrying over how long she could keep her daughter an innocent little girl, ignorant of the forces that saw only her inheritance.

Jared drove straight to the KingAir office. There was one small plane out front, ready to be taxied onto the runway. Desperate to limit any farewell scene, Christabel anxiously gabbled, "I'll take Alicia out to the plane while you notify the pilot we're here."

"She's asleep. I'll carry her. See you both strapped into your seats," he firmly countered.

"Okay," she agreed, realising his way might be easier, avoiding a spate of questions from a newly wakened Alicia.

The moment he switched off the engine, they were both out of the vehicle, Jared appearing as keen as she was to speed her on her way. There was no more talking between them. Whatever Jared thought of her decision, he was keeping it to himself and she was grateful not to have any argument from him.

They walked out to the plane in a silence that throbbed with all that remained unspoken. Having spotted them from the office window, one of the KingAir employees—the pilot?—raced out to catch up with them and be on hand to open the door and adjust the front passenger seat in the cockpit to allow access to the seats behind it. He helped Christabel into the small plane then stood back for Jared to lift Alicia into the seat beside her.

As he withdrew his arms from around her daughter, Christabel grasped his hand, wanting one last touch of him. ''Thank you, she said huskily. ''Thank you for everything, Jared.''

His mouth took on a wry twist as he answered, ''My pleasure.''

But there was no pleasure in his eyes. They were hard and flat and she had the quivery feeling that they were shielding a relentless drive to accomplish what he wanted accomplished. Which was probably to cut her out of his life as ruthlessly as she was cutting him.

''Fasten your seat belts,'' he instructed, moving his hand from hers to lock the front seat back into place. ''Take-off will be in five minutes.''

He closed the door and strode back to the office with the KingAir employee. The parting was so abrupt, she'd had no time to remind him about bringing the Cherokee to the airport. He'd remember, she assured herself. Though he might not want to remember anything else.

She sat in a pall of sadness, waiting for the pilot to come. Her chest was so tight, she needed the release of tears, but knowing instructions had to be given about her destination, she held back the flood that threatened. Later, when they were in the sky, she could give way to her grief for a while.

Her heart cramped when she saw Jared walking back to the plane. Alone. Was there trouble? More delay? Wrapped in dread of last-minute complications, she didn't realise his intention, even when he walked around the other side of the plane and hauled himself into the pilot's seat and closed the door behind him.

''Do we have a problem?'' she croaked out.

"None that won't get sorted," he answered, and switched on the ignition.

"Jared?" Bewilderment crashed into horror. "You can't..."

"This is my plane, Christabel, and I'm flying you to a safe place. As I promised."

"But you agreed..."

"The Cherokee will be brought to the airport to buy us more time, but when time runs out, my mother knows how to deal with your visitors."

Overwhelming panic. He was drawing his *family* into her mess! "Your mother doesn't know what she's dealing with."

"Doesn't matter. She knows I'm taking you somewhere untouchable. Where the only law is Lachlan's law," he said with grim satisfaction. "We deal from strength, Christabel, a strength that belongs uniquely to the outback."

"You don't understand their resources," she cried.

"Nor they ours," he retorted, totally unmoved by her protests, taxiing the plane towards a take-off position.

"Please, please listen," she begged. "You don't know what you're up against."

"But I will know, Christabel. Either from them or from you."

She heard the ruthless, relentless tone in his voice, knew the purpose he'd hidden behind the hard, flat eyes, and finally comprehended that Jared had no intention of letting her go before finding out everything he wanted to know.

"You might as well settle back and relax now," he instructed, facing the plane down the runway.

"Where do you think they can't get at us?" she asked in bleak resignation.

"King's Eden. We fly to King's Eden, Christabel. Tommy will monitor the airways. Nathan rules the ground. No-one can get to King's Eden without our knowing it, and if they come, it will be on our terms."

He was so sure, so confident. Maybe it was true. The Kings of the Kimberly virtually had a legendary status, having ruled their territory for over a hundred years. Were they impregnable in that majestic old homestead that had housed generation after generation of a family bonded to a hard, primitive land?

Primitive…the word stuck in her mind. For all Jared's sophisticated polish, he came from pioneering stock, people who fought for what they held, people who endured any and all adversity, people who survived and went on prospering.

She remembered the aborigines at Nathan's wedding, calling on the spirits of the Dreamtime with their didgeridoos. She remembered the timeless feel of the place, the daunting distances, the sense of a strong, unbreakable destiny embodied in Nathan King and his brothers, standing shoulder to shoulder, and the pride on their mother's face, looking at them with the bearing of a queen who knew she had given birth to kings…*kings of the outback*.

The plane lifted off, control in Jared's hands now.

Could this formidable family do it…break the chains of the Kruger juggernaut of power? She shook her head at the fanciful thought. Why should they when she and Alicia were not their responsibility? Nor did they owe her anything.

She had to tell them what they'd taken on, lay out

the whole picture for Jared to see not only what he was embroiling his family in now, but what he could expect in any future with her. Then he could decide if the fight was worth fighting.

His choice.

He'd overridden her choice.

She gave up worrying and let the blocked tears swim into her eyes. Jared might believe King's Eden was the perfect escape. He meant well. But Christabel couldn't believe it would really provide that. For her and Alicia it was the end of the road.

CHAPTER NINE

ELIZABETH KING waited for Vikki Chan's appraisal of the man who had come to her house. It was strange and rather disturbing, after all these years of widowhood, to find herself attracted—physically attracted— and excited by a man. She had believed such feelings had died in her when she'd lost Lachlan. Always to her mind, her husband had been one of a kind, unmatchable, yet Rafael Santiso had definitely put a zing in her blood.

Brilliant dark eyes zeroing in on hers, just as Lachlan's had, the power of the mind behind them reaching out, probing, challenging, so assured of commanding the situation, of dominating. Aristocratic Spanish, she'd thought this morning, taking in his elegant features and fine, upright figure. Argentinian, she knew now, and wondered if he came from a family who had owned one of the great cattle ranches in South America. There was that sense of unyielding mettle about him...but it was probably foolish to compare him to Lachlan.

A dangerous man, Jared had warned, a master of manipulation, trustee of the multimillion-dollar Kruger inheritance, and Christabel's daughter, Alicia *Kruger*, not Valdez, was the heiress. For over two years Christabel had been on the run from Rafael Santiso and the influence he wielded, and Christabel was not a fool. Her enigmatic behaviour was now answered, and given the story she had told Jared, her fears were certainly not groundless.

Yet to Elizabeth, even the sense of danger had a special exhilaration to it…the need to be on her guard, to be alert and ready to counter-challenge with her own power. She couldn't remember when she'd last felt quite so *alive*. It gave her an enormous buzz, knowing Rafael Santiso was waiting on her veranda, waiting on her pleasure, immune from any force from him.

She heard Vikki returning down the hall, and her heart lifted in anticipation of the old housekeeper's judgment. "Well?" she asked.

Vikki Chan entered the kitchen smiling, her eyes twinkling in amusement. "He is not used to being thwarted. But he is very quick, Elizabeth. In the blink of an eye he changed his intimidating manner to appealing charm."

"But he did try to walk over you initially."

"Frustration momentarily clouded his vision, but he is adept at reading people. He checked himself even as he began his demand for you, sliding it into a request."

"Your personal feeling about him?"

The shrewd black eyes didn't miss anything. "He is a mandarin."

Elizabeth frowned over the old Chinese term for a government official. The picture didn't fit for her.

"A red coral button mandarin," Vikki elaborated. "A wily governor and an efficient general."

"He's in charge of a vast financial empire," Elizabeth reminded her.

"A trustee, not an emperor."

"Christabel doesn't trust him. Such power can corrupt."

"I felt no evil in him. Neither did you, Elizabeth. You are drawn to him." Her all too wise eyes crinkled as she added, "You changed into the coral shift to match him."

Elizabeth laughed. "Does nothing escape you, Vikki?"

"He came alone. That is interesting, is it not?"

"We shall see. Bring refreshments out in about ten minutes."

"You don't wish to invite him inside?"

"No. Christabel regards him as the enemy. Until I am convinced otherwise, he will not be a guest in my home."

She was conscious of a rush of adrenalin as she walked down the hall to the front door. It *was* interesting that he had come alone. Her secretary had reported that all three men had come to her office at four o'clock, undoubtedly having discovered from Alicia's teacher that their quarry had left with Jared long before the end of the school day.

Elizabeth had deliberately gone home after she heard Jared's report from King's Eden. Let Santiso chase after her, she'd thought. How he did it would tell her more about him. He'd weighted his presence with the Swiss accountant and the German lawyer this morning, and again at four o'clock this afternoon. Now it was after five and he'd come alone. Elizabeth surmised a lot of thinking had been done in the past hour.

She opened the door. He stood well back from it, half-turned towards the view over Roebuck Bay, and he was no longer dressed in a suit. As he swivelled to face her, Elizabeth had the wild impression of a toreador, flexing his lithe muscular body and flaunting his virility.

Maybe it was the open-necked white shirt and black trousers, or the flash of sexual challenge in the magnetic dark eyes, or the sense of power tightly coiled, ready to be unleashed…whatever…the male animal impact was much stronger than before, and Elizabeth felt her stomach curl in response.

It was totally irrelevant that this was a man in his sixties, his thick black hair threaded with silver, his face lined with years of maturity. He exuded an immensely powerful sex appeal, and Elizabeth was suddenly certain he knew it and this was deliberately switched on for her.

"Mrs. King…" He offered his hand, even as she noted his voice had taken on a richer timbre, not so clipped and coolly controlled.

"Mr. Santiso," she replied, meeting his hand with hers and feeling an astonishing frisson of electricity on her skin as he fanned it with his thumb.

"Since I find that your son has flown off with Christabel and her daughter, I am at a loose end here in Broome," he went on, his eyes projecting a pleasant opportunity as he added, "I was wondering if I could persuade you to join me for dinner tonight."

Elizabeth withdrew her hand and floated it in a graceful invitation towards the table and chairs on the veranda. "An attractive suggestion, Mr. Santiso, but I shall need some persuasion. If you'd like to sit and enjoy more of the view here…"

"I've taken the Nolan Suite at the Cable Beach

Resort. It has a private dining room. I'm told the sunset from there is spectacular.''

"Indeed, it is. And I tend to think you'll be seeing many sunsets if you're waiting for Christabel and her daughter to return to Broome." She smiled and stepped purposefully towards the table, remarking, "From this side of the peninsula we enjoy the moonrise."

He laughed and followed her. "I take it you are conceding there is more than a professional connection between your son and Christabel."

"Jared is very dear to me, Mr. Santiso. He has been very dear to me for over thirty years." She settled on the chair at the far side of the table and raised an eyebrow at the man who presumed she could be won in bed. "Do you imagine the pleasure of being in the Nolan Suite with you would make me forget that?"

He grinned, totally unabashed. "You are, without a doubt, the most exciting woman I've ever met."

"Then why don't you sit down and pursue my acquaintance, Mr. Santiso?" Elizabeth replied, ignoring the absurd leap of her pulse. He had to be flattering her. Such a man could have his pick of any number of beautiful, clever and *younger* women.

He regarded her speculatively, still on his feet behind the chair at the opposite side of the table. "Why do you not believe me?"

"Because you're here for a purpose and I am not that purpose."

"Christabel must feel safe with your son."

"I believe she does. But she does not feel safe with you, Mr. Santiso."

"Rafael. My name is Rafael."

"I know."

"May I call you Elizabeth?"

"If you wish."

"I was entrusted with the responsibility of keeping the child safe. On Alicia's eighteenth birthday, she will inherit six hundred million dollars." He paused, watching her reaction. "I see you are not surprised, Elizabeth."

"Jared informed me of that fact two hours ago."

"And he is still intent on keeping them...*safe*?"

"We are not without means," she said with dry irony, knowing full well that six hundred million dollars dwarfed the wealth the King family could lay claim to. Yet there were resources that money couldn't buy, and inadvertently Elizabeth's eyes flashed that confidence as she added, "This is not your world, Rafael. It is ours."

"The Kings of the Kimberley," he mused softly. A whimsical little smile lingered on his mouth as he moved over to the balustrade between the veranda posts and turned his back to the view, dominating her vision as he faced her.

"I came to satisfy myself about your family. That is my purpose, Elizabeth," he stated directly. "I have known about Christabel's connection to your son since it started...months ago. I knew of her visit to King's Eden for the wedding of your eldest son. And on Monday morning I received the report that suggested that an intimate relationship had developed."

Was this true? He'd had Christabel watched all this time? Or had he gathered this information since his arrival today?

"Did you come to stop it?" she probed, wanting him to reveal more.

"Do *you* want it stopped?" he countered.

"I believe Jared wants Christabel more than he's ever wanted any other woman, and none of the barriers she has raised have turned him away. Believe it or not, the child's inheritance will be totally irrelevant to him. Some things can't be stopped."

"And you will stand behind your son."

She nodded. "His brothers, as well."

"Such a fortune draws more problems than prizes," he warned.

She was well aware of the power and politics attached to the Kruger cartel, the control they exerted over the diamond and gold markets, plus virtually every precious stone in the jewellery business...except pearls. The pearl farms of Broome produced the best in the world and were owned by Australian families.

"You cannot threaten our business, Rafael," she slid at him. "We would fight any attempt at interference and I have no doubt that supply and demand would come down on our side."

He shook his head. "No threats. I simply state the reality of the situation. The inheritance is more a curse than a benefit. It's not going to go away, Elizabeth. You will be loaded with the problems it brings."

Somehow we'll deal with them, Elizabeth thought, feeling more sympathy with Christabel than she'd ever felt before. Besides, this was not Europe. If Christabel wanted to stay with Jared, the outback had a way of protecting its own. Alicia would be insulated here from those who wanted a bite of her inheritance.

The question was...where did Rafael Santiso stand in this? What were his interests?

"If the inheritance is more a curse than a benefit, why do you stay in charge of it?"

His mouth tilted self-mockingly. "I'm addicted to problem-solving."

"Yet you allowed Christabel to run in fear of you. Do you call that solving a problem?"

He cocked his head slightly to one side, deliberating over his reply, possibly assessing its believability. This was the crux of the conflict between them and both of them knew it. It had to be resolved.

"She had cause for fear...but not from me," he stated, a harsh edge to his voice. "There were those whose interests were best served by poisoning her mind against me. As a result, she was resisting my efforts to keep her and the child safe, which made the situation more difficult."

He shrugged, and his tone slid into irony. "One cannot enforce trust. I saw it would be an easier task to facilitate her escape from the Kruger network, which she viewed as a prison."

"You planned it?"

"And directed it, every step of the way. The diamonds she has used for currency, the people who bought them from her, the bodyguards she never knew were watching over her. I can prove this, Elizabeth."

"Whether you can or not, she has still lived in fear of you," she tersely reminded him.

"I could not change that, and escape was her

choice. It gave her the sense of freedom she wanted," he sharply retorted. "If she had reason to fear me, do you think I would have allowed her any possible alliance with your family?"

"I don't know. You're here now."

He visibly relaxed, leaning back against the balustrade, his eyes taking on a warm velvety glow. "I like the connection. I'm liking it more all the time, Elizabeth."

"I think you have more explaining to do," she said flatly, not allowing any softening towards him.

He made an elegant open-handed gesture. "The reality was…Christabel's and Alicia's very carefully orchestrated disappearance served two purposes. It removed them from very real danger and left me free to deal with those who were contesting Bernhard's will."

"Is the danger now over?"

"There will always be the danger of kidnappers, but I'm satisfied that the house of Kruger has now been cleared of…malcontents." There was a ruthless glitter in his eyes as he curled his mouth around that last word. "Factions who want to shift the rules will undoubtedly form from time to time." He smiled. "But I am a very good watchdog."

And much more, Elizabeth thought, sensing the drive and commitment that took this man wherever he chose to be. There was almost a devil-may-care air in his smile, and she knew intuitively he thrived on danger, as well as problem-solving. Maybe it was that quality that made him so exciting.

"We would make good partners, Elizabeth," he said softly.

She lifted her gaze to his and once again was hit by the sexual challenge he threw at her. "Partners in protecting Alicia?" she tossed back, struggling to contain her response to him.

"Partners in every sense. You know it. It's in your eyes. How often in a lifetime does one look at a person and know this? It is rare, Elizabeth. It has never happened for me before today."

"I find that hard to believe, Rafael."

"I am a widower. I loved my wife with a young man's love. Much passionate emotion. But you...you I feel are my true partner. I would have fought your husband for you if he was still alive."

Lachlan...for a moment Elizabeth's heart felt torn...but Lachlan was gone.

Vikki suddenly emerged onto the veranda with a tray of refreshments. Had only ten minutes passed?

"Why don't you sit down, Rafael?" Elizabeth invited again, needing more time to think.

He looked at Vikki, accepted the inevitable delay in his purpose and moved to take the chair on the opposite side of the table.

Elizabeth thought of the long lonely years of her widowhood, thought of the years still ahead of her. Her sons didn't need her any more. They'd found partners. There would be grandchildren, but would they fill the empty places in her life? Lachlan's blood line would go on. There was really nothing left to achieve.

Rafael could be lying. A master manipulator, Jared had said. But what harm could one evening with this man do? She was not about to be seduced, not mentally nor emotionally nor physically. One evening alone with him committed her to nothing, except taking a chance she wanted to take.

"Thank you, Vikki," she said as her old friend and housekeeper unloaded the tray. "Don't prepare any dinner for me. Mr. Santiso has invited me to join him for the evening at the Cable Beach Resort. In the Nolan Suite."

She smiled into the eyes watching her from across the table, eyes gleaming with brilliant satisfaction. It isn't as easy as that, Rafael, she silently promised him.

"I daresay he'd like to show me the Sydney Nolan paintings that give the suite its name."

CHAPTER TEN

THEY were so calm, so confident they could handle anything—Jared, Nathan, even Miranda, Nathan's wife, serenely serving coffee. They weren't the least bit perturbed by the call that had come through at six o'clock, giving an update on the situation in Broome.

Christabel wanted to scream at all three of them that they didn't understand how Rafael Santiso worked. She knew how his evening with Elizabeth King would end. He'd be here tomorrow with Elizabeth's blessing and he'd walk right in to King's Eden, not having to breach any defences whatsoever.

Then he'd mastermind taking her and Alicia back out. All for the best, of course. A man who could persuade Bernhard Kruger into appointing him sole trustee of the inheritance could persuade anyone to do anything, and he had six hundred million reasons for doing so. Probably more by now, with his talent for wheeling and dealing.

The thought of returning to the prisonlike mansion in Amsterdam, or the Greek island fortress, set off a convulsive shiver, shaking the coffee cup in her hand. It clattered on the saucer as she set it down.

"Perhaps coffee isn't a good idea. Keep you awake," Jared remarked, rising from his chair at the dining table. "Would you like to go for a walk, Christabel? Some fresh air and exercise before you turn in for the night?"

"Yes. Yes, I would," she gabbled gratefully.

"I'll look in on Alicia," Miranda offered.

"Thank you," Christabel clipped out, jumping to her feet before Jared reached her chair, too agitated to remain still a moment longer. "Should she wake…"

"I'll sit with her," Miranda assured her with a warm smile. "Your daughter is a pleasure to be with, Christabel. I hope I can bring up our child as well as you have Alicia."

The tall, beautiful blonde was just visibly pregnant, and it was obvious both she and Nathan would be very loving parents. For a moment Christabel felt a savage stab of envy. Even if Laurens had lived, he would have been useless as a father. Worse than useless. Damaging. Whereas Nathan would be just as good and kind and caring as Jared…Jared, who still didn't see that Alicia's inheritance made everything abnormal, or was being stubbornly blind to the problems it encompassed.

She nodded to Miranda. "You're very kind." And she had been, ever since they'd arrived at King's Eden, taking Alicia under her wing, showing her around the homestead while Christabel had spelled out her situation to both Jared and Nathan.

Neither man had made light of it, yet she had been disturbed by the calm way they had accepted the facts, proceeding to make plans to ensure that her choices and decisions were respected. It was as though they took this outcome for granted, and Christabel was half-fooled into believing they could make it happen, until Elizabeth's call had revealed

Rafael Santiso's insidious manoeuvring, going straight for the head of the family.

Jared's hand fell lightly on her shoulder and she turned blindly into the curve of his arm as he drew her with him out of the dining room. Yet not even his physical warmth and strength could comfort her.

"It will be all right," he murmured, hugging her more tightly to him. "My mother's not a fool, Christabel."

She would never have described Elizabeth King as a fool, but Rafael Santiso could pull the wool over anyone's eyes, however shrewd and smart they were. "She doesn't know him as I do," she said flatly.

"One thing our family knows rather well is the art of survival," Jared assured her. "We don't give up. Never have."

But they could give way, Christabel thought despairingly.

It was a clear night outside. No storm today, except the one that had flown in from Europe, bringing the darkest clouds of all. She looked up at a sky full of brilliant stars and thought of the diamonds in her safety deposit box at the bank in Sydney. No chance of getting to them now. The running was over.

She had just this one last night of freedom. Santiso would come tomorrow. He and Elizabeth King would make Jared see that she and Alicia didn't belong here. A simple story leaked to the media would show the King family fast enough that their lives wouldn't be their own any more if they chose to keep the Kruger heiress under their roof. The man was ruthless and relentless in pursuing his own ends. And once he had them back under his control, would they die in an accident like Laurens?

"Let's walk down to the river where the marquee was set up for Nathan's and Miranda's wedding," she said impulsively, remembering that was where she had first felt Jared's arms around her, his body moving in tune with hers as they danced together.

"Being on the run is no kind of life for you, Christabel. Nor for Alicia," Jared said quietly. "I know you're frightened of it but a stand has to be made."

She didn't answer. What point was there in railing against the situation he'd forced upon her? It was done and couldn't be undone. She had one more night with him. That was the only consolation she had, and talking wasn't what she wanted.

She slid her arm around his waist as they strolled down the slope to the flat beside the river. He rubbed his cheek against her hair, and her heart turned over at the loving tenderness expressed. He really did care about her. Her fear had triggered all his protective instincts, and she realised his need to stand between her and her enemies had driven his actions today. She couldn't blame him for being the man he was.

"Did you think the inheritance would make a difference to what I feel for you?" Jared asked, a low throb of passionate emotion in his voice.

"It hasn't touched you yet," she answered reluctantly. "It probably seems unreal to you. But it's very real when you live with it, Jared. It...*dominates*... everything."

"You would choose to live without it."

"If I could."

"Which was why you kept running."

"Yes."

"And the longest you've stayed anywhere has been in Broome."

"Yes," she sighed, knowing she'd brought this disaster upon herself by staying too long.

He paused their walk, turning her to face him. "Because of me, Christabel?"

She reached up and laid her hand on his cheek, wanting the skin-to-skin contact with him, longing for more. This was the day of truth. There was no longer any reason to hide anything from him. In a heady rush of release, she spoke what was in her heart.

"I've never felt what I've felt with you. I shouldn't have let it...take hold of me so much...but you were there...and I couldn't put you out of my mind... couldn't resist having what I could of you."

"It's the same for me," he murmured, covering her hand with his and guiding it to his mouth, pressing a kiss on its palm, then sliding her fingers along his lips, over his chin, down his throat to the open V of his shirt, clearly craving her touch as much as she craved his.

"I can't bear not to have you," he said gruffly.

"Then have me. Here...now...all night long," she invited recklessly, both of her hands flying down the buttons of his shirt, wanting it shed, wanting all their clothes shed. "Help me," she cried. "I don't want anything between us."

She whipped off the T-shirt and shorts she wore and he was just as fast in stripping himself, incited by her urgency, her need to recapture what they'd shared before. Her heart was pumping fiercely as she revelled in the sight of his naked body emerging from the trappings of civilisation. Primal man, she thought wildly, strong and hard and vital, poised to claim her as his woman in this place of ancient earth with a universe of stars overhead.

She wanted this so much, so terribly much. It was how it should be—simple, direct, as elemental as the earth and the sky, timeless.

He reached for her, and she slammed against him, exulting in the squash of her breasts against the muscular breadth of his chest, the hard pressure of his arousal against her stomach, the rocklike steadiness of his thighs. Her arms wound around his neck as she went up on tiptoe, her mouth seeking his, and he met it with a kiss that ravaged her soul.

This was her man. It was as though every cell in her body thrummed with recognition of it, rejoicing in the miracle of having found this brilliant sense of rightness. She kissed him back with a feverish passion for all she could have of him, wanting to fill her senses with him, to absorb the whole physical wonder of him and hold it within her forever.

She strained as close as she could, rubbing her body against his, loving the exciting friction, the yielding of her soft flesh to his hard masculinity, the warm skin contact, the slight roughness of his body hair. Her hands caressed the strong column of his neck and roved over his shoulders and down his back, revelling in the smooth delineation of muscles tensed in holding her, binding her to him.

And she wanted to be bound, wanted to be taken and possessed, wanted to possess him. "Stand here,

Jared," she commanded in a fever of desire. "Stand here and let me take pleasure in you."

"Christabel..."

It was a husky whisper of longing and love and she felt his hands clench in her hair as she slid down his embrace, adoring his body with kisses, feeling his stomach contract under the softly erotic brush of her lips, rubbing his hardness between her breasts, clasping his taut buttocks as she took him in her mouth.

He groaned as she knelt between his thighs, his whole body tensing at the rhythmic caress of her mouth, and he lifted her hair, wrapping it around him like a fan of silk, taking a compulsive sensual excitement from it as the throbbing need for each other became more and more intense.

With an anguished cry, he hauled her up, then knelt himself, spreading her legs across his thighs as he rocked back on his heels, then bringing her onto him, plunging himself into her so hard and fast it was shockingly glorious, the sensation of his deep penetration and her sheathing him, holding him inside her. She wrapped her legs around his hips and arched back over his supporting arm, wanting the full length of him pushed as far as it was possible, revelling in the sheer ecstasy of encompassing the absolute extent of his male power.

Just as she sighed in blissful satisfaction, he leaned forward and began kissing her breasts, swaying her from side to side as he took each one in his mouth, drawing them into spiralling peaks of pleasure, possessing them as he reinforced the other more intimate possession, rolling her around him.

The sweet flow of climax came in exquisite waves,

the rocking from side to side accentuating every ripple of it through her body. Her limbs were going limp. She was hazily conscious of her hair brushing the ground, their bodies bared to the night, the stars overhead pulsing their myriad pinpricks of light at her.

Then Jared rose onto his knees, lifting her with him, before lowering her onto the ground and looming over her, and she knew it was time for him. She did her best to move with him and he didn't seem to mind that her body was languorous. His control amazed her and she thought he must be the best lover in the world—the pleasure King—still inciting intense rolls of blissful sensation in her as he drove towards his own climax.

She loved him—all of him—and when she felt him spilling himself inside her, it seemed like the culmination of her entire life, the fulfilment of what she was born for...to have this man, to share herself with him, to be joined like this in the deepest intimacy there could be between a man and a woman.

They hugged each other, rolling onto their sides, prolonging and extending their togetherness, savouring all the contact they could have with each other; kissing, stroking, totally absorbed in immersing themselves in the communion of touch.

It was Jared who spoke. Christabel would have been content to be with him in silence. To her, it was best, simply feeling him as a beautiful entity who belonged to her, to whom she belonged in this time and place, untouchable by anything else. But he spoke, and connected them back to a world she didn't want to think about.

"Marry me, Christabel," he softly pressed. "I can't imagine my life without you."

It stilled the whole momentum of her silent loving. A chill seeped into her bones. She couldn't bear to *start* imagining a life without him. It would happen soon enough. Couldn't they have this night without bringing the future into it?

"We were made for each other. You know it," he insisted, sliding her hand up his body and holding it over the strong beat of his heart.

She sighed, trying to ease the frozen tightness in her chest. "Ask me tomorrow night, Jared," she pleaded. "Not now."

For several moments she felt the rise and fall of his breathing and willed him to let the question pass, not wanting to face the conflict that would rob them of this all too short, peaceful idyll. But she sensed the gathering of purpose in him, even before he rolled her onto her back and propped himself over her, determined on pursuing the issue.

"Why not now?" he asked, gently raking her hair back from her face, intent on seeing all he could of her face, her expression, making evasion impossible.

She stared up at him, hating the circumstances that made accepting what he offered too heavy a burden on her conscience. "I can't tie my life to yours until I know what Rafael Santiso wants. What he's come for," she prevaricated.

"What do *you* want, Christabel?"

"I'm not a free agent, Jared. Alicia is my child and I will not give her into the care of anyone else."

He frowned. "I wouldn't expect you to. Though I'd be happy to adopt her and share the responsibility of parenthood with you. I would do everything in my power to protect her and give her a good home.''

Marriage…adoption…legal ties Rafael Santiso would undoubtedly see as possible threats to his trusteeship. And Jared was no pushover. He was demonstrating right now his will to fight for what he believed in, and he had the proven ability to run a multimillion-dollar business. Given a fair playing ground, he might even win against Santiso, but she was certain the Argentinian wouldn't play fair and Jared had too much integrity to play dirty.

''Alicia does like me, you know,'' he said persuasively. ''I'm sure I can win her acceptance to my being her dad.''

Being Alicia's *father* could very well lead to his death.

She sucked in a deep breath to calm the fearful flutter that thought evoked, then reached up to trace his lips with feather-light fingertips, desperate to recall the sensuality they had been wrapped in before. ''I think you'd make a wonderful father,'' she readily conceded.

''Then say you'll marry me, Christabel.''

''Please…let me think about it, Jared.'' She moved her hand to his ear, caressing the inner coils. ''Give me tonight to…''

''No.'' He shook his head, dislodging her touch. His voice hardened. ''This time I won't let you slip away from me as you did on Sunday night, leaving me with nothing but the memory of how it had been between us.'' His eyes blazed down at her. ''Tell me what's wrong with my proposition.''

The mood had changed. Irrevocably. Christabel

recognised there would be no more lovemaking tonight unless he got his own way, and she couldn't agree to a marriage with him.

"I'm cold, Jared." It was true enough. Her heart felt like a block of ice. "I want to get dressed. Let me up."

He hesitated, hating the evasion, wanting to maintain his dominant position over her, yet force was not his style. It never had been in all the time she'd known him. Persuasion, persistence, determination, yes...but not force. Even today he had not forced her into his plane. He had simply taken charge of flying it to a destination of his choice, doing what he believed would work best for all of them.

He rose to his feet, a proud magnificent man bristling with barely leashed aggression. He offered her his hand to help her up but she didn't take it, sensing he meant to lift her into his embrace and press her into the surrender he wanted. She rolled aside and lifted herself, springing to her feet at a safe distance from him.

"You won't trust my hand?" he challenged harshly.

"It's not a question of trust," she flashed back at him, then realising his hurt—all the hurt she had inflicted on him with her silence—she laid out the truth he refused to see. "I'm poison to you, Jared. I'm like a black widow spider. Bad enough that I've taken what I have from you. If you married me, I'd consume your life."

"I'm prepared to take that risk, Christabel."

"I'm not."

"Then why put off saying so until tomorrow?"

"Because I'm selfish and greedy, and I wanted more of you before tomorrow came."

Tears welled into her eyes and she tore her gaze from his, overwhelmed by a hopeless sense of defeat. She saw a piece of her clothing and snatched it off the ground, pulling it on in swift, jerky movements.

"Nothing is going to change tomorrow," he stated, puzzled by her time limit.

"Wait and see," she threw at him bitterly, hunting around for the rest of her clothes.

"I've done too much of that, Christabel," he retorted fiercely. "Tell me what you expect to happen."

"They'll come," she grated out, hating the inevitability that hung over her, dressing herself with a sense of savage protection against it as she told Jared what she anticipated. "Your mother will bring them. Santiso will persuade her. One way or another, he'll persuade all of you that it's better to let him take Alicia and me back into his custody."

"I'll never be persuaded of that," he declared vehemently.

Fully dressed again and feeling more armoured to face his arguments, Christabel squared her shoulders and looked straight at him. He was still carelessly naked, his entire being so focused on fighting her conviction, she was instantly caught in the tension emanating from him, her own nerves snapping at the intensity of the conflict he would not stand back from.

"It won't be your choice, Jared," she said quietly. "It will be mine."

"You'd deny me the right to choose the life I want? *With you*, Christabel, whatever it takes and wherever it takes me. It's what I want above everything else.''

His voice was furred with the passionate emotion he was pouring out to her and she felt it curling around her heart, squeezing it. ''I can't live with that sacrifice,'' she pleaded. ''Don't ask me to.''

''Even if you go with Santiso, I'll follow you. I won't give up.''

''You may kill us all if you don't, Jared,'' she cried, deeply agitated by his resolve.

''Kill?'' he echoed incredulously.

''The man I married, Alicia's father, stood in the way of Rafael Santiso's ambitions. He was blown up in a boat.''

It jolted the powerful flow of his will. ''You said it was an accident.''

''It was officially declared an accident. I don't believe it. I have no proof but I don't believe it. Don't get in Santiso's way, Jared. I'll never forgive myself if you do.''

While he was still distracted by the shock of her claim, she turned and started up the slope to the homestead, forcing her legs to move away from him and keep moving.

He had to let her go.

That was the ultimate truth.

And fighting it was fatal.

CHAPTER ELEVEN

JARED let her go.

The spectre of murder held him still, its ramifications swirling through his mind as he watched her walk away from him, trudging steadily up the slope to the homestead, a lonely figure bearing a dark knowledge, moving back into a darkness there was no escape from. Not for her.

He wanted to pluck her out of it, to promise her a different life with him, but he knew they would be empty words to her. Empty words to him, as well, until he could see a way past this final fatal barrier. As it was, he realised his continual pressing of the attraction between them must have been a torment to her all these months. It would be a gross act now to subject her to more pressure. He had no ready answers to ease her pain.

He'd forgotten her husband, dismissed him as irrelevant once he knew he'd died before Alicia was born. Five years—ancient history, he'd thought, while it had been five years of living hell for Christabel. And there was no end to it. No end to the Kruger fortune and the power behind it. That was a truth he couldn't dismiss.

He watched her until she was swallowed up by the darkness of the night. For several moments he was gripped by a haunting sense of loss, and a cold, cold loneliness pressed in on him. He looked up at the stars and felt the distance of them, unreachable yet there, twinkling their invitation to those who would dare cross space to get to them, dare anything to conquer the void.

A strong surge of determination burned through him. He would not accept that he and Christabel were ships passing in the night. He had taken it upon himself to bring her and her daughter to King's Eden, to stop her running. He would not let Santiso win. If there had been murder done, as Christabel believed, then any further threat of it had to be lifted and dealt with.

At least now he understood—why she ran; why she had tried to deny the attraction between them; why she'd given in to it, if only for a limited time; why the time—to her mind—had to be limited; the wretched weight she'd been carrying on her conscience about involving him in her life, a weight she'd wanted to put aside while having this one last night with him.

He understood that, too…the compelling need to feel all there was to feel between them while she still could. It wasn't selfish or greedy. It was as natural as breathing, the wish to extend the life of something beautiful, something he knew would never come his way again.

He believed she knew it, too, that what they shared went too deep to ever find with anyone else. It wasn't wrong to take what she could of it. She'd given him as much as she took.

But Jared had no intention of letting it end here. He set about picking up his clothes and putting them on. Christabel had her own brand of integrity. Not hurting others was high on her list. Perhaps that was a woman's way, doing her utmost to save those she loved from being harmed. But letting a predator win only put off other evil hours. The harm would come anyway. It had to be stopped.

Fully dressed again, he walked slowly up to the homestead, planning what he would do if Christabel was right in her reading of the situation. Fear might have distorted her view but he was not about to discount anything she believed. She'd acted on that belief with a determination that was stronger than her own personal desires. That said a lot to Jared.

The lights were on in the living room, Nathan and Miranda waiting in case they were needed. Jared glanced at the illumined numbers on his watch—21: 43. His mobile telephone was still in his shirt pocket. He paused by the bougainvillea hedge that surrounded the majestic old house and its immediate grounds, took out the telephone and hit the computerised code for the Picard home in Broome. He wanted to talk to his mother before he spoke to Nathan.

But it wasn't his mother who answered the call.

It was Vikki Chan.

"It's Jared, Vikki."

"She is not home yet, and she did not give me a time to be home," came the reply, cutting straight to the point of his call.

Jared frowned, impatient for another report. "Where can she be reached?"

"I think you should trust your mother, Jared, and wait for her to call you."

"Tell me, Vikki," he commanded curtly. "Don't come between us. This it too important to me."

"It may be important to your mother, as well."

"She is meeting with Santiso on my behalf," he argued.

"I do not think entirely, Jared. Rafael Santiso is a very attractive man and you may not see it as her son, but your mother is still a woman with a lot of life to live."

Jared's mind reeled over this new element. Never having met the man he had to give Vikki's judgment some credence on this point, but he found it extremely difficult to imagine his mother connecting to anyone after his father. He recoiled from the idea. Vikki had to be wrong. It might be a female pretence on his mother's part to fool Santiso into relaxing his guard with her. On the other hand, Christabel's conviction suddenly rang out loud and clear.

Santiso will persuade her. One way or another, he'll persuade all of you...

"Where are they?" he demanded grimly.

Vikki sighed. "He invited your mother to dine with him in the Nolan Suite at the Cable Beach Resort."

"She's gone with him to a private suite?" Even he could hear the edge of outrage in his voice.

"You have no right to judge what is right for your mother," came the terse reproof. "I remind you she respected your choice of Christabel, knowing very little about her."

"But we do know about Santiso, don't we?" he retorted angrily. "Christabel told us."

"Trust your mother, Jared. She is not a fool."

His own words to Christabel thrown back at him, yet his judgment of his mother was now severely shaken. *She does not know him as I do,* Christabel had replied, and those words burnt into his mind, building a belief that his mother *was* being fooled by a man who had no scruples in using anything to get what he wanted.

"I'll see what happens tomorrow," he said, ending the call, his mind already occupied with Christabel's other predictions.

He activated Tommy's telephone number, determined on building a safety net. "Jared here," he announced the moment Tommy answered.

"No news of movement yet," came the instant report.

"He's with Mum. In the Nolan Suite at the Cable Beach Resort, no less. And get this, Tommy. She finds him attractive."

"You're kidding."

"Vikki Chan's judgment. Want to knock it?"

A shocked silence. Both of them were acutely aware of the old Chinese housekeeper's closeness to their mother, and her astute summing up of any situation.

"Christabel called Santiso a master manipulator," Jared went on. "She expects him to persuade Mum to bring all three of our European visitors to King's Eden tomorrow. If that's in the wind, Tommy, I want you in Broome tomorrow morning to fly them out yourself. No charter pilot. You. We keep this in the family. Okay?"

"Right you are. I won't keep Sam out, though."

"She's family." Tommy's fiancée had been like a kid sister to Jared for most of his life. He'd trust her with anything. He was going to trust her with a vital part of his plan. "I have a job for Sam, too, Tommy," he said, and outlined the responsibility he wanted her to take on.

"No problem," his brother assured him. "Where do you expect this to end, Jared?"

"I don't know yet. I'm hoping to sort out the truth tomorrow. But the final outcome—I will not have the woman I intend to marry living in fear."

"I'm with you, Jared." Hard resolve in his voice.

"Thanks, Tommy."

Satisfied he had countered whatever persuasion Rafael Santiso was working on his mother, Jared moved forward, heading for the home that had sheltered the King family for over a hundred years. He paused at the front gate, feeling the spirit of those who had built this place and the legendary memories it embodied, the hospitality that had always been extended and the rules implicit in that hospitality.

Let Santiso come, he thought grimly. If the Kruger trustee and his cronies demonstrated any poisonous fangs, they would be cast out of Eden and left in a wilderness, the like of which they would never have experienced before.

It wouldn't be the first time a transgressor learnt at first hand the rigours of survival in the outback, gradually acquiring a new respect for life and the lives of others. All the money in the world was futile and meaningless on that journey. Lachlan's law had always delivered a punishment to fit the crime—justice not only done but seen to be done.

Jared decided he would like very much to give Rafael Santiso a taste of fear, a taste of feeling there was no way out *for him*. A couple of years of that might very well revolutionise his thinking, give him a true appreciation of what Christabel had been put through. Though he had to be certain such a course was warranted before carrying it out.

His mother's apparent vulnerability to the man was another issue. It nagged at his sense of rightness as he proceeded past the gate and on to the house. Surely her sharply honed instincts wouldn't play her false. He had never once felt out of tune with his mother. Never. Could she be so deeply deceived by Santiso?

As he'd anticipated, Nathan and Miranda were waiting for him, sitting in the big room that housed generations of choices in furniture—antiques, Asian influences, modern comfort, exotic collector pieces. Somehow they all melded together into a fascinating blend of people's pleasure.

His mother always sat in the armchair upholstered in scarlet silk brocade. He wished it wasn't empty tonight. Nathan occupied the huge black leather armchair that accommodated the length and breadth of his formidable physique. Miranda, whom Jared had walked down the aisle to his brother because she had no known father or family, eyed him worriedly from the sofa she favoured.

Was Christabel bereft of any family, as Miranda had been before marrying Nathan? There was so much he still didn't know. What of her life in Brazil, before she'd met and married Laurens Kruger?

"Christabel came back alone," Miranda remarked questioningly. "She asked about Alicia then took her leave of us for the night. She looked as though she'd been crying, Jared."

He winced at the grief he'd unwittingly caused her in cutting short the comfort of loving by demanding answers to his need. Still, better that he had a fuller picture of what had to be fought. He turned to Nathan who waited patiently to be informed, his sharp blue eyes trained on his youngest brother, aware of the complexities of the situation and what Jared wanted from it.

"There's more," Jared stated bluntly, and filled Nathan in on the latest developments, delivering a sharp summary as he paced around the room, too wrought up to sit down. "So how do you stand with this?" he finished, more belligerent in his demand than he meant to be.

"With you," Nathan answered calmly, pushing up from the leather chair, his height and solidity automatically emanating authority as he moved to clasp Jared's shoulder in a gesture of unison. "We'll take whatever action is called for."

Absolute support. Jared saw it in his eyes and felt his inner angst ease. They were one in this—all three brothers—as he had assumed they would be—their father's sons—but his strong sense of family unity had been rattled by his mother's apparent leaning towards the other side.

"What about Elizabeth?" Miranda asked anxiously, echoing Jared's own concern.

Nathan swung to answer her, his face expressing no inner conflict whatsoever. "We protect our own," he stated decisively. "That means Mum, too. If her judgment is...awry, what happiness do you think she'd find with him?"

Miranda shook her head. "It's so hard to believe. Your mother is..."

"Lonely," Nathan supplied. "Rafael Santiso heads

and holds together a financial empire. It takes a certain type of character to achieve that.''

He turned back to Jared, an ironic gleam in his eyes as he added, ''Whether she feels an echo of our father in him…or something else…who knows? There has been an empty place in her life for many years.''

For the first time an attraction made some sense to Jared…a man of unshakeable willpower, a man who challenged his mother…and he well understood *empty places*. He was grateful to Nathan for his perception. Human frailty he could accept.

''We tread carefully there, Jared,'' his big brother asserted quietly but firmly. ''Hold back any sense of humiliation if Mum has been deceived. We must leave her dignity intact. Did you make that clear to Tommy?''

''No. I was angry,'' Jared had to confess. His eyes ironically acknowledged his own human frailty as he added, ''I felt…betrayed.''

Nathan nodded his understanding. ''You've been closest to her. In the end, she'll put you first. I have no doubt about that. I'll call Tommy and talk it over with him. Okay?''

Jared was reminded of all the times in his boyhood when Nathan had *fixed* things for his little brother. He smiled in wry appreciation. ''I am grown up now.''

Nathan laughed, his eyes twinkling appreciation and acknowledgment of the fact. ''Just saving you time, Jared.'' He sobered and gestured to his wife. ''Miranda's right. Christabel had been crying on her way back from her walk with you…''

''I had to take care of business, but I would be obliged if you'll talk to Tommy. And thanks,

Nathan.'' He reached up and clasped his brother's shoulder, a lump of deep emotion welling into his throat. ''You never have let me down and it's good to know you're still here for me.''

''We're here for each other,'' he answered gruffly. ''Always.''

Jared found himself too choked up to speak. He lifted his hand in a salute to Miranda, spun on his heel and walked out of the room, carrying with him a multitude of feelings that made life all the more precious to him, feelings he wanted Christabel to experience when she joined her life to his.

When, he thought fiercely. Not *if*.

He strode down the hall to the bedroom wing where she and Alicia had adjoining rooms. He'd done all he could to cover contingencies. His brothers were on-side. King's Eden was King's Eden. Tomorrow would come, but first there was this night to get through and Christabel needed to be loved.

More than that.

He needed her to believe in his love.

And that took action, not words. Tomorrow he would show her how deep and enduring his love was, but tonight was for feeling it.

He knocked softly on her door, hoping Alicia was asleep in the next room and Christabel was not sitting with her. He waited for several long seconds. When there was no response, he knocked again.

Again no sound of movement. Was she cuddling her daughter for comfort, deliberately ignoring any intrusion on her privacy? He couldn't imagine she was asleep herself, though it was possible. He glanced at his watch. It was over an hour since she'd left him.

Then the door opened a crack. "Who is it?" came the husky whisper.

"Jared."

He heard the shaky expulsion of a long breath. "There's no more to say tonight," she said listlessly, the weary dullness of her voice transmitting the sense of everything being over, and her acceptance of it.

"I just want to be with you, Christabel," he softly pressed.

The door was held at a mere crack. Jared sensed the conflict tearing at her—to open up or close—and pushed to end it.

The door swung open. No resistance. No welcome, either. She wasn't immediately visible. A lamp on the bedside table was switched on, spreading a soft glow of light around the room. The bed was mussed, the pillow dented, evidence that she had been lying down.

He found her sagged against the wall behind the door, as though she no longer cared about anything, letting him do what he willed because it really made no difference. Her head was lowered in a beaten expression, her cheeks streaked with tears, her long hair in a tangle of disarray. She wore the white nightgown Miranda had supplied, a sexy satin slip, but there was no sexual awareness in the slump of her shoulders, and her eyes were closed, shutting him out.

He closed the door and gathered her into his arms. She seemed too drained to fight anything any more, letting him draw her body to his, dropping her head limply on his shoulder. He held her, gently stroking her hair, rubbing her back, hoping he was imparting warmth and comfort, trying to wrap her in a blanket of love that would soothe her inner anguish.

Eventually her arms slid around his waist and her body heaved in a long, ragged sigh. "I'm sorry it is...how it is," she said tiredly. "I never meant to drag you...or your family...into this."

"I know," Jared murmured. "I'm sorry you've had to bear so much alone."

"I have Alicia," she answered, resigned to the curse of the inheritance—the price of having the daughter she loved.

"Was there no other family of your own to help?" he gently probed.

She raised her head, looking at him with sad, washed-out eyes. "They did help...when I went back to Rio."

She broke out of his embrace, shrugging off his solace as she turned away and walked towards the bed, her hands waving futile little gestures as she explained further.

"Through family contacts I managed to sell some of my jewellery to get untraceable money, passports in a different name. But I knew they couldn't shelter me for long. My family was known. I had to leave them." She paused, half-turned, aiming a direct look at him. "Just as you must know...I have to leave you."

He shook his head. "Not for my sake, Christabel. And not because I might endanger your life or Alicia's, because I won't do that." He strolled towards her, holding her gaze with purposeful conviction. "Only if you want to, and I don't believe you do."

He saw the flash of naked yearning in her eyes before she veiled it with her long lashes. Even as she jerked her head forward in a negative protest, he reached her and swung her around to face him, to hold her more firmly.

"Jared…"

"No. No more talking. Say you must leave me to-morrow night if you decide that's how it has to be, but love me now, Christabel, as I love you."

He kissed her and her anguish turned into a passion that matched his. No persuasion was needed. The loving was too intense not to be believed by either of them, and for Jared, that was enough to carry them through whatever had to be done to assure them of a future together.

CHAPTER TWELVE

THE day Christabel had always dreaded through her years of running had arrived. It felt strange not running any more...just sitting, waiting, letting others take charge, trying to hold onto her belief that Jared could take care of everything when the men in suits came. The clock was ticking down. In less than two more hours they'd be landing at King's Eden.

Christabel found it difficult to keep fighting the waves of panic that knotted her stomach. She felt hopelessly distanced from the King women who emitted the same calm confidence as the men, blithely chatting over the breakfast table in the old homestead's huge country kitchen, as though there was nothing whatsoever to worry about.

Jared and Nathan had left them some time ago, intent on discussing some plan with the Aboriginal tribe members who lived on the cattle station, but still no note of anxiety crept into the cheerful conversation between Nathan's wife and Tommy's fiancée.

They talked of plans for the upcoming wedding to be held in Kununurra at the end of the wet season, progress on the house Samantha and Tommy were having built on a hill overlooking Lake Argyle—exciting things in normal lives—and while most of it floated past Christabel's tension-ridden mind, Alicia was gobbling it up.

From her five-year-old view, Miranda was a lovely

143

lady who reigned over a cattle kingdom, and Samantha—whom everyone called Sam—so bright and pretty with her copper curls, sky-blue eyes and friendly freckled face, was an exciting adventuress who could fly a helicopter. Both of them happily pandered to Alicia's avid interest in their activities.

Christabel wondered if the imminent visit of the men from Europe and what they represented seemed unreal to them. Though she recalled that Miranda had been in hotel management before marrying Nathan, so she'd be used to dealing with people from all walks of life, and Sam Connelly, as a charter pilot, would also be familiar with moneyed clients. Even so, Christabel doubted they'd ever met the like of Rafael Santiso, and he and Vogel and Wissmann were not coming here on a pleasure jaunt.

There was no safe place, she thought bitterly. Elizabeth King had been persuaded into bringing them to King's Eden, just as Christabel had predicted, and only the fact that Tommy was flying them in kept a measure of control in the family's hands.

"Well, I guess it's time for me to be going," Sam announced, surprising Christabel out of her assumption that the whole family was gathering to present a block of support.

"You're leaving?" It felt like a desertion, rattling what little confidence she had in what they could achieve on her and Alicia's behalf.

"Have to fly to the house to supervise some carpentry." She smiled warmly at Christabel. "Since you'll be occupied with the men today, I thought Alicia might like to come with me. I have a picnic lunch in the helicopter."

"Oh, could I please, Mummy?" Alicia cried, her eyes agog with excitement.

"You can contact me any time," Sam assured Christabel, patting the mobile telephone hanging from the belt of her jeans. "It's only a fifteen-minute flight if you want us back. But it sure would be fun having your daughter along with me."

"Yes, yes," Alicia pleaded.

It dawned on Christabel that the reason Sam was here was to take Alicia out of the Kruger equation, at least physically, until the conflict of interests was settled. For the past couple of hours she had been winning the child's trust and building her liking so the invitation would be accepted quite naturally—no frightening sense of being taken away by a stranger.

"It won't be a problem," Sam promised, her clear blue eyes shooting both sympathy and moral support as she pointedly added, "she'll be safe with me."

Safe…a weight lifted off Christabel's heart. Alicia, at least, would not be subjected to any trauma today. "Thank you," she said with deep gratitude before smiling at her daughter. "Promise you'll be good and do everything Sam says."

"I promise." She was off her chair and dancing around in wild eagerness.

Miranda held out a hand to her, laughing at the childish excitement. "Come and we'll get your hat from your room."

As soon as they were gone from the kitchen, Sam addressed the *real* issue. "I've known Nathan and Tommy and Jared all my life. You couldn't have better men on your side, Christabel. None of them will shy from doing whatever has to be done to ensure you and Jared can make a life together.''

She hadn't agreed to marrying Jared, or even sharing any more of her life with him. She tried to explain her position. ''There are…risks.''

''No risks, no prizes,'' Sam lilted back at her as though her own experience had taught her that being passive didn't get her where she wanted to go. She showed no concern whatsoever over *her* part in today's arrangements and seemed intent on soothing Christabel's fears as she chatted on.

''Tommy will be flying your visitors over the most inaccessible parts of the Kimberly—no roads, no vestige of civilisation, just ancient ranges and big, daunting, uninhabited country. He wants to impress on their minds how challenging it is to survive here, and how the sheer isolation of it can eat into one's mind and heart and soul. Amazing how quickly it can change perceptions and responses and values.''

''It won't mean anything to them,'' Christabel informed her. Money people were only interested in money, she thought cynically.

Sam cocked her head on one side, apparently considering her assertion. ''It can come to mean something in hindsight, Christabel, especially to those who underestimate what they're taking on when they come face to face with the outback. It's the land that rules, not men. It changes the terms.''

Christabel looked more sharply at her, sensing she was suggesting how Rafael Santiso might be dealt with. ''Are you saying…they may be kept here until they see things differently?'' she asked incredulously.

''Well, I expect they will learn something about

very basic values on this trip." She nodded some personal satisfaction. "I think your Mr. Santiso will be considering his decisions very carefully before this day is out."

Or he'd be abducted and given a learning experience? Christabel was still struggling with this concept. "Jared and Nathan and Tommy..."

"Won't allow you and Alicia to be victimised," Sam slid in, obviously delivering the bottom line.

"But..." Her hands fluttered in agitation. "...the repercussions."

Sam shrugged. "I tend to think it will just end up a different ball game. No repercussions at all. The Kings have their own way of protecting their territory and their people. Believe me, you're *safer* with them than you would be anywhere else."

Jared believed this. Strangely, Sam's conviction gave *his* belief more substance, probably because Sam wasn't quite so personally involved, though she was taking care of Alicia today. Maybe it was being outback bred that gave Sam Connelly this knowing confidence of how this unique part of the world worked.

Her words...*doing whatever has to be done*...kept echoing in Christabel's ears. Jared had been like that from the beginning, never accepting defeat, constantly edging forward even as she fought each of his intrusions in her life. He didn't give up. And from what Sam said, neither did Nathan or Tommy.

She had been so caught up in worrying about what Rafael Santiso might do to the King family, she simply hadn't considered what the King family might do to the man who had haunted her all these years. To use the outback itself as a weapon...a persuader...changing the terms...

She remembered very vividly the primeval feeling of the land she had flown over, the same sense of it here at King's Eden, and suddenly realised it *would* have to seep into and influence the nature of the people who lived here. She had felt it about Jared each time she'd seen him naked—a powerful primitive entity intent on claiming what he wanted.

Rafael Santiso had always seemed an unstoppable force—but the King family *were* a different breed to the men he was used to dealing with. The prospect of a head-on collision between them made her feel weirdly skittish inside and she was glad when Miranda and Alicia came back, immediately presenting the activity of seeing her daughter off in the helicopter with Sam.

It was good to listen to Alicia's excited chatter as they all strolled down to the landing strip beyond the big equipment buildings. Her little face was so wonderfully alive and carefree, untouched by the inheritance she knew nothing about. Christabel fiercely wished it could be kept that way, at least for enough years for her character to develop without the influences wrought by great wealth.

A normal happy child flew off with Sam Connelly.

Christabel couldn't help feeling apprehensive about what her daughter would fly back to and how it was going to affect her.

"It's all fixed so that Alicia will not meet the men you fear unless you decide it's okay," Miranda informed her as they watched the helicopter zoom off into the distant sky.

Christabel looked sharply at her. "How is it fixed?"

Miranda smiled reassuringly. "They won't be staying here. Tommy will fly them to his wilderness resort, which adjoins the cattle station. You were accommodated in one of the cabins for my wedding, weren't you?"

"Yes. But I thought it was closed during the wet season."

"It has resident maintenance staff. Your visitors will be housed in the resort homestead for the duration of their stay at King's Eden."

"I doubt they intend to stay long."

"Well, I expect that will depend on what happens at this morning's meeting, which, of course, will be under our control."

Christabel stared into the calm green pools of her hostess's beautiful eyes. There was not the tiniest trace of apprehension marring her serenity. The King family was arranging their chessboard for the battle ahead, holding Alicia—the queen piece—safe from any possible attack, moving the enemy king and his two rooks where *they* chose, making the opposition aware of the dominant factor of *their* ground, and Christabel suddenly wondered what kind of backup Jared and Nathan were arranging with the Aboriginal tribe.

Alarm streaked through her. So much had been arranged without any consultation with her, but what if Rafael Santiso had organised his own backup before climbing into Tommy's plane this morning?

"You don't know these men and what they're capable of, Miranda," she shot out, disturbed by a confidence that had no cracks to allow for other outcomes.

"I know *our* men," she answered feelingly. "I know what they saved me from and how effectively they did it. They are quite fearless in their strength, Christabel. That's something I don't think more *civilised* men meet with in their very *civilised* lives."

It was a different reflection of what Sam had said...the primitive element of survival running through them, taught by the harshness of an environment that demanded they be fit to endure anything. Maybe the land itself did change the terms and the King family could prevail over whatever forces Rafael Santiso mustered.

Still inwardly agitated, Christabel sought more evidence of their strength. "What did they save you from?"

Miranda grimaced ruefully. "From a man who was intent on ruining my life because I wouldn't play his game. He was the heir to an international chain of hotels, with the power of great wealth behind him. He thought he could use it to influence the King family against me." She shook her head reminiscently. "It meant nothing to them. So you see, the Kruger inheritance won't mean anything to them, either."

She hooked her arm around Christabel's, lightly pressing a sympathetic togetherness as she started them on the walk back to the homestead. "They will support you. Unequivocally. Through anything that's thrown at them."

"It's asking a terrible lot," Christabel couldn't help saying. "The inheritance won't go away and others will come."

"Jared loves you." Miranda's lovely green eyes glowed with secure knowledge as she added, "Nathan loves me. Tommy loves Sam. Each of them understands what it means to them. There is nothing in this world that would make them give up their women."

Christabel's heart quivered at the enormity of such deep, abiding love. Could she accept it, unequivocally, whatever came? She wanted to. It was what she had felt flowing from Jared last night, and her whole being yearned to love and be loved by him for the rest of her life.

No risks, no prizes.

Her gaze turned up to the homestead that had stood as an emblem of endurance for over a hundred years. It was beautifully maintained. The huge white roof glistened in the morning sunshine. The white veranda posts and the decorative iron lace that ran around the eaves lent it the image of a crown, majestically dominating the vastness of the land around it.

A crown for the Kings of the outback, Christabel thought whimsically, feeling they truly were kings of men, deserving of crowns. She hoped they would endure, that she wouldn't be the one to bring them down, that somehow something could be worked out so she and Alicia could live happily with Jared.

She loved him.

But whether the prize of love would be worth all the risks, only time would tell.

CHAPTER THIRTEEN

CHRISTABEL drew in a deep breath as the minibus from the King's Eden wilderness resort came to a halt. Jared's arm was around her waist and he gave her a quick hug, reminding her she was not alone. They were lined up along the veranda at the front entrance to the homestead, he and Nathan standing together, she and Miranda on either side of them, waiting to greet the visitors.

It was forty minutes since they'd seen Tommy's plane come in—forty very long minutes, knowing *they* were here. It was almost a relief to see the Kruger triumvirate alighting from the minibus, and something of an anticlimax that they weren't wearing suits. Their open-necked shirts and light cotton trousers made them look less intimidating but Christabel knew that was an illusion, and the black leather briefcases they carried gave the lie to any casual air they might adopt.

Rafael Santiso and Elizabeth King led the little procession through the front gate, Vogel and Wissmann following, Tommy behind them, shutting the gate with the air of a shepherd who had successfully herded his flock to the designated pen.

But he'd brought the wolf into the fold, Christabel thought, and with each step Rafael Santiso took towards her, she felt her nerves tightening and her hope for an agreeable outcome dwindling.

His black-eyed gaze skimmed the four of them

waiting on the veranda, pausing fractionally on
Christabel before turning back to Elizabeth who was
talking to him. A smile lurked on his mouth as he
projected interest in what she said. A smile...was the
King family a joke to him? Would he learn differently?

Her heart started fluttering as he stepped up onto
the veranda. Elizabeth introduced him to Nathan and
Miranda first. The Argentinian was not as tall or as
big as Nathan—more a match to Jared in build—but
he exhibited no sign of being the least bit intimidated
by Elizabeth's oldest son, and Miranda was definitely
greeted with a flash of male admiration, as though
this was a social occasion.

Jared he measured with sharper eyes, and his nod
as he moved on to Christabel seemed to express a
satisfaction that put her more on edge. How could he
be pleased about the aggression she could feel pumping through Jared? Stupid thought, Christabel railed
at herself. Rafael Santiso thrived on fights. The
tougher the opponent, the more pleasure in the win.

"Christabel...I'm glad to see you looking well."

His cultured, urbane voice sent a shiver down her
spine. She couldn't bring herself to make a reply,
glaring her contempt for his supposed caring about
her well-being. She felt like spitting at him.

One devilish eyebrow arched inquiringly. "Alicia
is not here with you?"

"No, she's not," Christabel snapped defiantly, and
the urge to puncture this charade of normal civility
bolted out of her control. "She's out of your reach,
Rafael."

Her fierce claim evoked only an ironic little smile.

"I see it is well past time to address the matter of trust."

"Well past time," Jared asserted, the subtle challenge in his voice drawing Santiso's attention back to him.

The brief interchange was broken by the introduction of Hans Vogel and Pieter Wissmann. Then Nathan was ushering them all inside.

Jared held her back, turning her into his embrace, his eyes boring into hers with urgent intensity. "I know you feel cornered. I also know you have the heart of a tiger. Together we can fight our way through anything," he declared with conviction.

The heart of a tiger? Was that what was pounding inside her? Through the whirl of apprehension in her mind came the thought—if ever there was a time to claw her way to freedom, this was it!

"I will fight, Jared," she promised him, and saw the leap of satisfaction in his eyes.

The big, formal dining room had virtually been turned into a boardroom for this critical meeting. When she and Jared entered, Rafael Santiso, flanked by Hans Vogel and Pieter Wissmann, occupied the far side of the huge mahogany table, the contents of their briefcases formidably stacked in front of them.

Nathan sat at the head of the table with Miranda on his left. Elizabeth sat at the foot of it with Tommy on her right. Two vacant chairs between Tommy and Miranda stood waiting for Christabel and Jared, directly across the table from Rafael Santiso.

Jared seated her between Tommy and himself. Miranda had set out jugs of iced water, and Christabel gratefully noted that the glasses around the table had

been filled. Her throat was very dry. She didn't want
to look at Rafael Santiso but pride made her face him,
and as Jared settled beside her and took her hand,
interlacing his fingers with hers, a strong surge of
rebellion poured through her *tiger* heart. She would
not let the Kruger trustee take over her life. She belonged with Jared.

"What business brings you to us, Rafael?" Jared
opened up, letting it be known that Christabel was
not to be singled out as a separate entity.

"Many serious considerations," he answered.
"First, may I say how pleased I am to have the opportunity of meeting the King family en masse like
this." He swept a look of pleasure around the table,
stopping at Tommy. "I presume your fiancée,
Samantha Connelly, has Alicia in her safekeeping."

"Yes, she does. Sam will keep her happy,"
Tommy rolled back at him, not the least bit ruffled
by the sharp intelligence behind the assumption.

"Alicia is unaware of her inheritance and
Christabel wants it kept that way," Jared stated, purposefully drawing Rafael's attention back to him and
throwing out a probing challenge.

"Impossible in the long term," Rafael countered.

"We aim to keep her free of it for as many years
as we can," Jared pressed.

Christabel felt the formidable power of the mind
that had manipulated the trusteeship being brought to
bear on the issue raised. Whatever he said would
sound reasonable. In all her dealings with him he had
never sounded *unreasonable*, which had made him so
impossible to fight. He spun a web that covered everything. Her skin crawled as she anticipated the first

set of strands, intended to wind around her in an inescapable net.

"An interesting proposition," he said *reasonably*, even with a hint of sympathy for the task. "Part of why I'm here is to assure myself of *your* capability of delivering what is needed...to ensure a relatively safe and happy life for both Christabel and Alicia."

It was the last thing any of them expected to hear and the arrogance of the claim was breathtaking. A sense of disbelief hung in the stunned silence around the table.

Christabel's mind spun at the boldness of such a strategy—evading any accountability on his part by putting the King family on the line. She leaned forward, a welling outrage demanding to be voiced, but Jared spoke first, squeezing her hand as he did so.

"That is not your business, Rafael," he stated curtly. "It's mine and Christabel's and Alicia's. You're not their guardian."

"I promised the child's grandfather I would keep her safe," came the equable reply.

"Thereby ensuring the Kruger inheritance is kept safely in your hands," Jared fired at him point-blank.

It stung, jerking Rafael's chin into a tilt of pride. "It *is* safe in my hands. Safer than in anyone else's."

"Fine." Jared belligerently tapped the table as he went on. "But you will not hold Christabel and Alicia hostages to your personal or financial interests." His hands cut a decisive scissorlike movement. "They're free of you now and they'll stay free of you."

Rafael leaned forward, his eyes glittering scorn. "But are they free of others, Jared? Do you imagine that *I* am the only one who has a personal and financial interest in the Kruger fortune? Alicia is a hostage to anyone who wants a bite of it.''

Jared leaned forward, boring in. ''You're the one Christabel fears most. You're the one she fled from.''

Rafael flung a hand out in brusque dismissal. ''A misconception.''

''Then clear it up, Rafael. Now!''

Jared sat back, ostensibly prepared to listen, but he left the air between him and Rafael Santiso electric with challenge. Adrenalin was pumping through Christabel. She seethed over the word *misconception*, all primed to pounce on any clarification she knew was false.

Rafael frowned momentarily as though gathering his thoughts, then with an open-handed gesture that suggested he had nothing to hide, he said, ''Let me explain to all of you that when Bernhard Kruger died, the arrangements made in his will were not to the liking of two powerful factions within the company. It was…a dangerous time.''

His gaze swung directly to Christabel. ''The precautions I put in place to protect you and Alicia were necessary. I know you felt imprisoned and you saw me as your gaoler.'' He shook his head ruefully. ''There was nothing I could do to alter your view. In effect, it was true. At the time, I believed it was the only way of discharging my duty as Bernhard's appointed trustee.''

If it was an appeal for *her* understanding, it fell on stony ground. Christabel stared back at him, unmoved. She was sure he had Laurens's blood on his hands, and it would only be a matter of time before he'd be planning Alicia's demise, as well.

He held her gaze, determined on getting through to her. Seeing her resistance he pressed, weighting his words with very deliberate purpose. "I was more aware than you were of how quickly, how ruthlessly, a life can be snuffed out when that life can influence what happens to a fortune."

Was he warning her? Threatening her?

He paused, looking for fear in her eyes? Christabel could feel the pulse beat in her temples but she would not bend to any pressure from him. Jared would stop it somehow. Jared and his brothers.

"Remember Laurens?" Rafael continued in a softer tone.

A taunting reminder that her husband was dead? That Jared, too, could be dead if she didn't come to heel?

"It was not an accident that killed your husband, Christabel."

The shock of that open admission jolted her into speech. "I never believed it was," she flared at him, then couldn't stop the churn of truths that had driven her to take the course she had. "To me the only question was…who was behind his removal from the Kruger power pyramid? And the answer…" She stood up, needing to fight, to force him into more admissions. "…the answer, Rafael…was written in the outcome."

Her fists pressed onto the surface of the table as she leaned over it, pouring out the line of logic that couldn't be refuted by the man who'd profited most by Laurens's death.

"His death served *your* purpose so very neatly, putting you at the head of the South American net-

work in *his* place, which brought you directly into
Bernhard's inner circle. It gave you the chance to win
his confidence and you do that so well, Rafael...
winning people's confidence. You got it all, didn't
you? And before Alicia is eighteen, no doubt you'll
find a way to eliminate her, as well.''

The blistering indictment had no visible effect on
him. He sat quite still.

There was a breathless silence all around the table.
A pin dropping would have been a shattering sound.
Christabel realised she was trembling and abruptly sat
down, breathing hard as though she'd run a long race.
Jared took her hand, pressing warmth and reassur-
ance.

Hans Vogel coughed and leaned forward, looking
as though he was about to protest. He was a heavy-
set man, bald and bespectacled, with a bullish authority that didn't suffer fools gladly. Christabel
glared at him, refusing to be reduced to a mere cipher
he could roll over.

Rafael Santiso simply raised his hand and the lawyer settled back again. "So *I* was the bête noir all
along," he softly mused, then looked inquiringly
around the table. "And this you all know—
Christabel's belief that I had her husband murdered?"

Nathan, Miranda, Jared and Tommy all remained
silent, watching him, giving him nothing to hit off.

Elizabeth spoke, shock evident in her tone. "You
didn't inform me, Jared."

"I didn't know of it until last night," he answered
quietly. "And it was irrelevant to the action being
taken this morning. I wanted you to bring them here.
It's the best place to deal with the situation. We were

all agreed on that and since you now know the score..." He swung his gaze to the man who'd charmed his mother "...let him answer the charge."

To Christabel's ear, there was a relentless beat in Jared's voice that carried the message it was Rafael and his men who were cornered, not her and Alicia. She squeezed his hand, her courage lifting with having him so staunchly on her side.

Rafael Santiso shook his head, as though in disbelief at finding himself in this position. His running glance from Nathan to Tommy left him in no doubt that the King brothers were sitting in judgment on him. Christabel wondered if he was remembering the country he'd flown over to get here, whether the isolation of it was hitting him now.

Then his gaze targeted her, snapping her mind back to red alert. He thought she was the weak one to be worked upon, twisted around. Not today, she silently vowed.

"You hid your suspicion well," he remarked, displaying no hint of acrimony over her accusations. "I would have corrected it, or asked Bernhard to correct it, had I realised you believed me to be behind Laurens's death."

"As you well know, Bernhard is *beyond* speaking for you," Christabel retorted, showing her scepticism.

He shrugged. "The train of events will speak for him. As it was, you were deliberately cocooned from what was going on. You were heavily pregnant. There was concern for both your health and the child's."

Another *reasonable* stance. Christabel would have none of it. She attacked straight back. "When I spoke of my doubts about the accident to Bernhard, he dismissed what I said out of hand, Rafael. Why should I even begin to believe what you say of that time?''

"It was men's business, Christabel. You were a young woman of twenty-two. You lived under Bernhard's wing for almost three years. From your own experience of him, do you really imagine he would discuss something so personal as the murder of his son and heir with you?''

He paused, giving her time to remember the old man's patriarchal arrogance and his limited view of his daughter-in-law, then pressed home a truth she could not deny. "Your only function to Bernhard Kruger was to be a good mother to his grand-daughter.'' His voice softened as he added, "In that, may I say, you have always excelled.''

Christabel instantly bridled.

"I advise you that repeating Bernhard Kruger's attitude towards Christabel is not acceptable,'' Jared inserted coldly. "At this point, facts will serve you better than any sentiment which reinforces her position as Alicia's mother and ignores the respect due to her as a person in her own right.''

Once again she was surprised at how closely attuned Jared was to her feelings and took deep comfort in how at one they were.

Rafael raised a challenging eyebrow to Christabel. "Have I accurately summed up your situation in the Kruger household?''

"Yes. Before and after his death when *you* took over,'' she answered bitterly, all the old resentments at being treated like a brainless chattel burning through her. "I was very young and very naive to have ever married Laurens in the first place. But then you banked on that, didn't you?''

He actually looked surprised at her reading this much into the part he'd played. "It was your choice, Christabel.''

"Under pressure from my parents." Her eyes hotly accused him of being the source of that pressure. "You brokered a deal with my father. Don't bother denying it. He confessed it after I fled to Rio to get help from my family. A bigger better jewellery business in exchange for a daughter to beget another Kruger heir."

There was a rustle of movement from her side of the table and she sensed more than saw the heightened interest her words had sparked. She had not spoken of this to anyone, shying from revealing her past foolishness. But it was pertinent here.

Aware she was adding more fuel to the fire she was building under him, Rafael instantly sought to cool it down. "You know it is the way the old families arrange it in South America. I was delegated to offer the bride price. That is all I did. The choice was still yours. And you seemed taken with Laurens."

"You've already commented on how *young* I was, Rafael. I was flattered. Overwhelmed. But you knew what kind of man Laurens was and what I was being led into."

He shook his head. "For all I knew of you then, you could have viewed it as an advantageous marriage. Many women would see it as a passport to a life they envied. You made the decision, Christabel."

"And I'm sure you found it advantageous—a South American bride, approved of by Bernhard

Kruger. Another little fortuitous connection on your way up the ladder.''

He lost patience with her argument, tersely replying, "It had no bearing on my situation, which only changed after Laurens was gone."

"And then you came into everything. My point entirely," she fired at him.

"Except it's based on a false premise," he snapped. "I had nothing to do with Laurens's death, Christabel."

"Prove it!"

The demand rang through the tension in the room, seeming to bounce off the walls. Anger showed clearly on Rafael Santiso's face, an anger that laced his voice as he bitingly asked, "Are you prepared to listen now?"

"By all means lay out your *train of events*," she threw back at him.

He swept a dark burning gaze around the King family. "I understand that Christabel needed to voice the suspicions that have festered for so long, but that is all they are—suspicions. Justifiable in her situation, but unjustified by any proof. Please keep that in mind."

He turned to the lawyer beside him. "Hans, take them through what was done."

The lawyer was in his seventies, a long-time aide in the Kruger camp and undoubtedly privy to many secrets. As much as Christabel disliked him, Rafael's confidence in handing his defence over to the older man did intrigue her enough to command her attention.

"Bernhard instantly suspected that the boat which

exploded and killed Laurens had been sabotaged,"
Vogel related tonelessly. "He offered a large reward
for the identity of the saboteurs. The information
came in. The men directly responsible for Laurens's
death volunteered the name of the man who'd hired
them. He revealed a conspiracy within the Kruger network, a certain pressure group that was planning a
division of interests which would be highly profitable
to those involved."

He paused, his light blue eyes zeroing in on
Christabel. "It was centred on our South African connections, nothing to do with South America."

"The boat blew up in the Caribbean," Christabel
swiftly reminded him.

"The Caribbean is an international playground,"
came the instant rebuff. "A place for international
gossip amongst jetsetters."

She had to grant him that.

Hans Vogel continued with barely a pause, his eyes
boring through the cynical reservations in hers.
"Laurens heard a rumour of the conspiracy at a party
and asked some indiscreet questions instead of bringing what he'd picked up to his father. You were married to him. You must know he liked to pump himself
up, wanting to make himself a bigger man than he
was. It turned into a fatal flaw."

Yes, she did know, Christabel silently conceded.
Laurens would have exulted in telling his father
something Bernhard didn't know, showing off, prov-
ing how important he could be. "Do I know any of
the conspirators?" she asked.

Hans Vogel shrugged. "I doubt it. I do have the
entire list of names in my office safe. Not with me. I

can assure you Rafael Santiso is not one of them. But I can produce the reports if you so wish. It is impossible, however, for you to speak to anyone on the list about these circumstances."

"Why is that?"

"Regrettably, all of them have died…in accidents," he said very dryly. "The hand of justice, is it not?"

The hand of an old man wreaking vengeance on those who'd agreed to the murder of his son! She should have been shocked but oddly enough it all seemed very distant to her—another life, another world, one she didn't want to return to.

Pieter Wissmann, the Swiss accountant, sat forward. He was a pale thin man in his fifties who always carried an air of precision. "If you want objective confirmation of what occurred, following on from Bernhard's investigation …"

He looked at Nathan, Tommy, then directly at Jared. "As men of business, you will appreciate that financial figures tell their own story. The rearrangement of the South African operation is quite dramatic, directly related to the elimination of corrupt connections and the building of a new network. If you wish to examine the records on this, I can make them available to you."

Christabel frowned over the sheer weight of the revelations, her mind torn at having her own long-held belief in Rafael Santiso's guilt crushed. The offering of such confidential information was extraordinary. The list of the conspirators' names, their deaths, which could be officially confirmed, the money trail…she had to be wrong about Rafael's involvement in Laurens's death. There was too much evidence pointing elsewhere. *Firm* evidence, not suspicions based on steps that could have favoured him in his rise to the trusteeship of the Kruger inheritance.

Jared stirred beside her. "Do I understand, from both of you…" he said slowly "…that everything pertaining to Laurens Kruger's death was cleared up and acted upon while Bernhard Kruger was still alive?"

"Yes. The conspiracy, once uncovered, was excised with maximum efficiency," Hans Vogel replied.

"The reorganisation took longer but it was in place and running to Bernhard's satisfaction before he died," Pieter Wissmann confirmed.

"Thank you. We appreciate your candour and cooperation in offering this sensitive information," Jared assured them respectfully, then leaned forward, resting his forearms on the table, his gaze trained on Rafael Santiso. "I have two questions," he stated in a tone that demanded satisfaction.

"Ask them," Rafael invited brusquely, emitting the attitude that he could answer anything at any time.

"Given that the conspiracy had been comprehensively dealt with…why was it so dangerous for Christabel and Alicia when you took over after Berhard's death, to the point of your becoming their *gaoler*?" He let Rafael's own word hang for a moment. "And given Christabel's obvious wish to be free of you and all you represent…why didn't you respect *her* choice, *her* decision…as you did when she married Laurens Kruger?"

Jared paused, then quietly added, "Please keep in mind that Christabel has the right to choose the life she wants, and as Alicia's mother, she has the right to choose what she feels is best for her daughter. That is *our* concern here. We are yet to understand *your* concerns…the purpose behind this uninvited and un-welcome intrusion on a life that literally has nothing to do with you.''

Again there was that relentless beat in Jared's phrasing, a quiet but very real menace underlying the words that spelled out the heart of the matter in un-equivocal terms, and what had to be answered.

Even as Christabel felt a strong surge of love for this man at her side…her soul partner, her cham-pion…she looked at Rafael Santiso and wondered if he sensed what he was facing—*no escape*.

No escape, she kept thinking, amazed that those words could now apply to the seemingly all-powerful figure she had fled from.

Maybe she and Alicia could be safe here.

Or was she assuming too much, too soon?

CHAPTER FOURTEEN

JARED knew he was facing the most testing experience in his life. He'd dealt with many a cutthroat businessman in the pearl trade, but these three men were on a different level altogether. They accepted, apparently without question, Bernhard Kruger's ruthless *elimination* of the conspirators responsible for his son's death. No weighing the degree of guilt. A complete sweep.

While Christabel had not known of these extreme measures, she had certainly picked up what these people were capable of—power that recognised only its own law of maintaining power, whatever that took.

And while Rafael Santiso did not have her husband's blood on his hands, could her instincts be right about him where Alicia was concerned? Would he acknowledge that the child was not *his* to be controlled as it suited him? Even if he did, could he be believed?

Jared watched intently as the Argentinian considered the questions put to him. His mother was attracted to this man. Vikki Chan had not given any caution against him. Both women had finely tuned instincts that would normally pick up on any shading of integrity. But Jared had too much riding on the outcome of this confrontation to have blind faith in their judgment.

''Perhaps I was overzealous in protecting

Christabel and Alicia, but I cannot regret what I did,''
he said with an air of honest assessment. "If my precautions were extreme, it was because the responsibility of their safety sat heavily on me, knowing what
had happened to Laurens, and I was very conscious
that Bernhard's mantle did not fit my shoulders.
Those who had respected his power were all too prepared to test mine.''

A different man at the helm—a deputy instead of
the old master—yes, Jared could appreciate the pressure to perform would be on.

Hans Vogel broke in, his thin mouth curling in dis-
gust. "Bernhard was not even in his grave before the
challenges to his will began from those who led powerful factions within the Kruger organisation. As far
as they were concerned, the king was dead and the
throne was for their taking, regardless of Bernhard's
legal appointment of Rafael as sole trustee of the inheritance."

His bullish face turned to Christabel. "You owe
Rafael more than you know. But for him…"

"Enough, Hans!" The silencing hand was lifted.
"The prison Christabel found herself in was not of
her making." Rafael turned his gaze to her, his expression slightly puzzled, searching. "The fear you
had of me must have made it worse. I saw hatred for
what I stood for, resentment of what I enforced,
but…" He shook his head. "…fear I did not read."

"I would not give you any more leverage over
me," Christabel replied, pride ringing loud and clear.

Rafael nodded thoughtfully and looked back at
Jared. "I've already said it was a dangerous time after
Bernhard died. There were many in the organisation

who believed he had become unhinged from his illness and grief for his son. They had expected him to appoint a board of trustees to manage the inheritance, not just me. Alicia was certainly perceived as a vehicle to gain more control.''

His eyes took on a mocking challenge. "What would you have done, Jared…if you were me? Let Christabel and her daughter run loose to be snatched and ransomed? Risk Alicia's life? Her death would have instantly fractured the structure Bernhard had set up—an advantageous situation to some.''

Jared recalled that he himself had taken command yesterday, not consulting Christabel about flying them to King's Eden, simply doing it, believing he knew best how to assure their safety. This place, too, could become a prison. The difference was…Christabel did not fear him as she'd feared Rafael. She *wanted* to be with him.

"Like you, I would have thrown a blanket of protection around them,'' Jared answered slowly.

"As you have here,'' Rafael was quick to point out, his eyes lighting with satisfaction.

"But I am not the oppressor,'' Jared instantly countered. "To Christabel, you were and are, extending a life she hated. It's a question of values, Rafael. You were looking after the inheritance, regardless of any quality of life for her.''

"At least she *had* life.''

"An intolerable one.''

His head tilted in a concessionary nod. "I did come to realise that, Jared, when Christabel effected her escape. It was a desperate act, given she knew the dangers of being without any security around her. At first

I thought…'' He shrugged. ''Once I found her jewellery was also gone, I knew it was a personal bid for freedom, rather than running to another Kruger camp.''

He leaned back in his chair, a musing little smile on his lips. ''So what would you have done then…if you were me? Let her go? Tried to find her and bring her back? What, Jared?''

It came to him in a lightning flash what Rafael Santiso had done, and why he was here now, meeting the King Family. Relief poured through him. Christabel and Alicia *were* safe, and his mother and Vikki Chan had not been fooled.

He expelled a long breath. He looked at Christabel's long-time nemesis with a new respect for the man of integrity he actually was, a man who shouldered his responsibilities with utter commitment, yet tempering that commitment with a humanity Jared had to admire. The only thing Rafael had overlooked was Christabel's fear of him, unrecognised, partly because she had hidden it from him, partly because he hadn't known how she'd painted him in her mind.

''Do you have the reports with you?'' Jared asked.

Respect instantly flashed into Rafael's eyes.

Understanding flowed between them, man to man on equal footing.

Rafael picked up a Manila folder, thick with documents, from the pile in front of him and slid it across the table. ''Much of this contains summaries. If you want more detail, Hans will supply it.''

Jared nodded, picking up the file and rising to his feet. ''I'd appreciate it if you'd run through your protection procedure with my family while I speak to Christabel privately.''

''I shall do that and give any explanation they require.''

''Thank you.''

Rafael smiled. ''It is good to know at first-hand the mettle of the man who is taking on...whatever has to be done.''

Jared turned to help Christabel out of her chair. She came unresistingly but looked totally bewildered. ''It's all right,'' he assured her. ''We'll come back after we talk.''

''Before you go...''

It snapped their attention back to Rafael. He was looking at Christabel, a powerful intensity in the eyes trained directly on hers.

''I did not know of your fear of me, Christabel, but it did serve you well in your travels, keeping you cautious and not drawing any untoward attention to yourself and Alicia. I want you to know that in the years you've been gone, I have stamped my authority on the Kruger organisation, and I no longer see any danger coming from within. From outside is another matter, but we will discuss that later.''

She shook her head, confused by the turnaround from enemy to ally. Jared took her arm and steered her from the dining room, wanting to get her out of the highly charged atmosphere that swirled with the memories of all she'd been through. She needed to feel free, to follow her own heart without fear, and Jared knew he could give that to her now.

He took her onto the veranda that skirted the homestead—fresh air to breathe, a view that had no boundaries in sight—the vast tracts of King's Eden stretching to the horizon and beyond. *The land of my fathers,* he thought, feeling a well of pride in his heritage. Because he was who he was, and all that was imbued in him, he would have Christabel and keep her, and that was a glorious feeling.

"What are these reports?" she asked anxiously. "What are we doing out here, Jared?"

"Do you still believe Rafael Santiso caused Laurens's death?" he asked, scanning her eyes for any hint of doubt.

She expelled a heavy sigh and made a wry grimace. "No. But I still think he's dangerous."

"Yes. To anyone who crosses the line he draws. But not to you nor Alicia, Christabel," he assured her with absolute certainty.

"How can you know that?" she cried, the old fear still fluttering.

"Because he's been protecting you all along. That's what these reports are about. He let you think you were free because you wanted so badly to be free, but he watched over you all the way to here, Christabel. And he came now because of me, to see if I'm good enough to take over the watch from him."

Her feet faltered to a halt. She swung to face him, her agitation intense. "He could have plucked me and Alicia back any time? Is that what you're saying?"

He nodded. "From Rio onwards would be my guess. He would have put your family under surveillance the moment he realised you'd fled with your jewellery."

The colour drained from her face. "All this time," she said faintly.

"To ensure your safety as best he could, Christabel, while giving you the freedom you craved."

She shook her head. "I can't believe it." Her gaze dropped to the file he held. "Show me. I want to see what he did."

Jared curved an arm around her shoulders. "There's a table on the western veranda. We'll sit down and you can read all you want."

She moved with him, dazedly repeating, "All this time...he knew?"

"Yes. And I'd imagine—smoothed the path for you wherever he could."

They sat where his family usually gathered to watch the sunset—the end of the day. It was only a little past noon, yet the sense of the end to a long, long road for Christabel evoked a similar feeling of being able to relax now.

He didn't read the reports. He listened to Christabel's comments on them, her initial incredulity stretching into an awed understanding of how Rafael Santiso had facilitated her *escape*, as well as taking every precaution he could for her and Alicia's continued well-being, without any overt oppression or constriction.

The passports in the name of Valdez were not forged, as she had believed. Rafael had organised that the name of Kruger be legally changed to the one she'd chosen. Wherever she had sold her diamond jewellery, *his* people had ensured she received what it was truly worth. She and Alicia had never been without bodyguards hovering close by. Even in

Broome, the caravan next to hers had been occupied by Rafael's *watchers*.

There was also a report on the King family—their history and their holdings—and an assessment on their possible reaction to Alicia's inheritance. The judgment was that it would have little or no influence on the life paths they had taken. The Kings of the Kimberly were deeply rooted in their territory and would not shift from where they were.

"You see?" Christabel commented ruefully. "The intrusion into your life and your family's has already begun, Jared." Her eyes searched his, needing reassurance. "Do you really want to take this on?"

He nodded. "Whatever comes, Christabel." He reached across the table and took her hand, enfolding it in the secure strength of his, determined on resolving everything for her to the best of his ability. "They're here to lay out the situation with Alicia's inheritance—Wissmann to deal with the money side, Vogel to deal with the legalities, Rafael to advise on protection."

She sighed, her eyes filling with pained apology. "I had it so wrong."

"Not with me. We have it right together, Christabel." He smiled, wanting to soothe the angst she felt. "Remember Vikki Chan?"

"Yes."

"A very wise old woman, Vikki. She said of you— and I remember the words exactly—*There is a strong wall of integrity in Christabel Valdez which will not be broken. I think she does, and will always do, what she believes is right.*"

A little burst of pleasure brought a golden light to

her beautiful amber eyes. "I felt her taking stock of me but…to read so much?"

"I've never known her to be wrong about people. So I'm asking you now. Can you…" He held her gaze, pouring all his love for her into his voice. "…do you believe it's right…"

He had to hold her.

"Believe what?" she asked shakily as he stood and scooped her up into his embrace.

"I need to hear you say it's right for us to marry, Christabel," he declared with a passion he could no longer contain. "That nothing could be more right because that's what I feel and I have to hear it from you…"

It wasn't a command. It wasn't an appeal. It was a burning certainty in his heart as he spoke the words he wanted her to say.

"…because it's what you feel, too."

CHAPTER FIFTEEN

SIX months on...

"Mummy looks so-o-o beautiful," Alicia breathed on an ecstatic sigh.

Vikki Chan smiled at the child's focus on her mother, who did indeed look as beautiful as a bride should. Truly Jared's bride, Vikki thought indulgently—a tiara of pearls holding her veil, a magnificent necklace of pearls around her throat and pearls studding the diamond pattern on the guipure lace of her strapless bodice. A big silk taffeta skirt billowed out from her hips—extravagant, graceful and lustrously sensual. Altogether, Christabel presented a vision that surely had Jared's cup of pleasure running over.

She was right for him—her wonderful little boy who had become such a man. Tommy was a delight. Nathan was Lachlan all over again. But Jared had always been her favourite—so sensitive and perceptive and receptive, his mind alive to the life in everything, almost Chinese in his appreciation of how nature shaped both good and bad for reasons of its own, the unseen influences that nevertheless did influence important outcomes—winning or losing.

Jared knew how to win. Instinctively, intuitively, he got it right. He had the gift for it. And he certainly looked the winner this evening—so tall and handsome and splendid in his formal silvery grey suit. Even the high peaked white collar of his dress shirt and the silk cravat looked perfect for him. A truly magnificent man. He made her feel very proud.

And having the wedding here in Broome for the whole town to see her boy and his bride...it was an occasion to savour in the days to come, talking it over with her old friends. A touch of honour, too, having Chinese lanterns hung around the grounds. It was a fine choice having the wedding at the Mangrove Hotel, out on this big lawn overlooking Roebuck Bay. Soon the moon would rise....

"Alicia King," the child lilted, trying out the name. She looked up at Vikki, her big brown eyes sparkling with excitement. "Now that Mummy's married to Jared, I'm not going to be Alicia Valdez any more. I think King sounds better, don't you, Vikki?"

"It is a fine and honourable name, Alicia, and a great blessing to be one of the Kings of the Kimberly. They are a family to be proud of."

"I love having a family," the child declared feelingly. "Now I've got a father like all the other girls in my class at school, and when Tommy and Sam fly me back to King's Eden after the wedding, Miranda said I could help mind her baby."

Vikki nodded to herself. People, not money, gave the real riches of life.

"I hope Mummy and Jared have a baby," the child rattled on. "Then I'd have a brother or a sister. Do you think they will, Vikki?"

"In time, little one. We must always wait for good things to happen. There comes a right time and that is the best time."

*   *   *

"Let's sit down, Miranda." Sam rolled her eyes at her sister-in-law. "I *need* to sit down."

Miranda laughed and accompanied her to the closest vacant table. As Christabel's matrons of honour, they'd been standing for a long time, throughout the wedding ceremony and then the photograph session, and Sam was four months pregnant, though it barely showed. It didn't show at all in the princess line dress Christabel had chosen for them, and the midnight blue colour was definitely slimming. Flattering for her own figure, as well, since it was only a month since she'd given birth to Matthew and she wasn't yet back in shape.

"All I can say is, thank heaven the morning sickness is over. Pregnancy does not suit me," Sam declared as she sank onto a chair. "I get so tired all the time."

"This, too, will pass," Miranda advised, taking the chair beside her.

"Where's your gorgeous baby boy? I need a reminder of what's at the end of this."

"Nathan has him, parading him around the guests."

They both laughed. Nathan doted on his son.

"Tommy's going to be the same. He's so cock-a-hoop that we're having a girl."

"Well, it will be the first one born to the King family for three generations."

Sam grimaced. "I always wanted to be a boy myself. I'm not good at the female thing, Miranda."

"Nonsense. Boy or girl, I think you just have to let them follow their own nature and enjoy them for what they are. Besides, you've been marvellous with Alicia and you've said yourself she's a delightful little girl.''

They both turned their gaze to Christabel's daughter who was chatting away to Vikki Chan, her vivacious face alight with excitement. She'd been a bundle of excitement all day, being a flower girl at her mother's wedding and so happy to be getting Jared as her father.

''You're right. I do enjoy Alicia,'' Sam conceded.

''Please God we never get some nasty investigative reporter connecting her to the Kruger heiress,'' Miranda murmured. ''She's such a lovely natural child.''

''Good thing Rafael had fixed up the Valdez identity so it was legal. It made everything easier for them.'' Sam nodded to where Rafael Santiso and Elizabeth stood together, watching the bride and groom while they enjoyed a private tête-à-tête. ''He's covered his tracks here, too, with his personal interest in Elizabeth.''

''I doubt that has much to do with covering his tracks,'' Miranda said dryly. ''Rafael is seriously courting her, Sam.''

''So it would seem. What does Nathan think?''

''He thinks she should go for it. What's Tommy's reaction?''

''If it makes her happy…''

''Look at her. She's glowing.''

''Fatherhood definitely suits you,'' Tommy declared, his eyes dancing in amusement at the sight of the itty-bitty baby snuggled in the crook of his brother's arm.

Nathan's towering height and big frame made him look like a giant compared to the smallness of his newborn son, yet he was a very gentle giant with Matthew, and Tommy was actually moved by the love so clearly emanating from his older brother.

"It's great, Tommy." Nathan grinned. "And it's great you're having a daughter. Got any names picked yet?"

"Sarah heads the list at the moment."

"It's been quite a year, hasn't it? Three weddings, a son for me and a daughter for you on the way."

"Plus an adopted daughter for Jared."

Nathan laughed. "Miranda heard her practising her new name as they were getting ready for the wedding. She was reciting Alicia King in front of the mirror and looking very smug about it."

"What do you think will happen when she gets to eighteen?"

"Best thing would be to give that inheritance away. Have Rafael administer it for charities. Alicia won't need any of it with Jared as her dad."

"And Christabel doesn't want a bar of it. I'd guess her influence will soak in over the years."

"Sure to. She's one very strong lady."

Tommy shook his head over the traumatic train of events that had eventually landed Christabel in Broome. "Hell of a thing—what she went through."

Nathan looked over the milling crowd of guests to where his youngest brother stood with his bride—the woman he'd fought for and won. "She's got Jared now," he said quietly. "I think for Christabel, he more than makes up for everything she suffered in the past." His vivid blue eyes twinkled at Tommy.

"I'd have to say our kid brother wins the white knight award."

"Oh, I don't know. We did pretty good for Miranda, don't forget. Saved her from a king rat."

"True. And I'm glad Rafael Santiso didn't turn out to be another king rat. I suspect he's going to sweep our mother off with him."

They both turned to assess what was happening on that front.

"You know, Nathan, for an older guy, he's certainly got a pouncing panther air about him."

"Mmm...not unlike Dad in many ways."

Rafael Santiso felt he had been very patient. It was time for Elizabeth to decide.

"So," he said, eyeing her with mocking challenge. "We had Tommy's wedding four months ago. Nathan's son has been safely born. Miranda is handling motherhood without any panic whatsoever. The planning for Jared's wedding has reached its culmination and is currently being perfectly executed. Your youngest son is now married. Samantha's baby is not due for another five months and I shall point out that unlike Miranda, Samantha has a mother of her own to see her through to the birth."

He arched an eyebrow. "Is there any reason you cannot leave the Kimberly and fly to Greece with me?"

She affected surprise. "I thought you were returning to Europe."

He shrugged. "Athens is on the way. I hold a small Greek island in trust. Very private. Very beautiful. It is the perfect place for relaxation after such a busy six months."

"It has been busy."

"And frustrating," he said darkly.

Her magnificent eyes twinkled seductively. "I've never been to a Greek island."

His heart swelled with hope. "You have only to say yes."

I can, with a free conscience, put myself first now, Elizabeth decided. How it would be with Rafael, she didn't really know—such a different kind of life—but she wanted to try it, wanted to explore the feelings he stirred in her. It wasn't too late to take a new path, she thought. It was never too late. She had been static for too long. Life was to be lived.

She smiled at Rafael, thinking how exhilarating it was for a woman to feel desired by such a fascinating and desirable man. "I can't think of any family need to keep me here, so yes, I will go with you."

"You will?" His handsome Latin face broke into a triumphant grin.

Nothing to lose and everything to gain, Elizabeth told herself, and made the decision firm. "I will."

Jared curved his arm around Christabel's waist as they stood at the fence edging the grounds of the hotel, facing out to where the full moon was rising, a glowing red ball pushing slowly up from the horizon beyond Roebuck Bay.

"Happy?" he murmured.

She smiled. "You know I am. Though I do wonder

how your mother feels about us living in Picard house. It's been hers for so long.''

''Now that I have you, she's passing it to us, Christabel. She'll be gone by the time we come back from our honeymoon.''

It surprised her. ''Where is she going?''

''With Rafael.''

''She'll really leave all her family to be with him?'' A flash of concern in her eyes. ''It's such a high-intensity life he lives, Jared.''

He smiled, his confidence in his mother's ability to rise to any challenge stronger than ever. ''Invigorating, Vikki says. And she predicts he'll treat her like a queen.''

Christabel released a long contented sigh. ''I have to admit he's been good to me. Amazing in taking care of the problems with Alicia.''

''You don't mind giving up your family in Rio?'' he asked quietly.

She shook her head. ''They want the money. When I went to them for help, they thought I was mad to leave. It was Rafael's hand behind the scenes that made them give the help I needed. It was the same when Laurens proposed marriage. They thought only of the money.''

The eyes she lifted to his held no regrets. ''My life is here with you. So is Alicia's. She loves *your* family, Jared. And so do I.''

The last little niggle about all the decisions they'd made in the past few months was erased. He nodded towards the bay. ''It's starting.''

Christabel swiftly turned her attention to the unique phenomenon that was special to Broome. It was most spectacular during the equinoctial tides of March and September when the sea could rise and fall ten metres. At such an extreme low tide, and if the sky was clear as it was this evening, the pools of water stretching across the exposed mudflats reflected the light of the moon, providing the illusion of a staircase—a magical staircase opening up from the huge glowing sphere as it rose above the horizon.

The first red bars were appearing now.

A night to remember, Christabel thought, for so many wonderful reasons, and this...what she was watching now...seemed like a reflection of what Jared had done, hauling her out of darkness and setting her feet on a path with him, a path where every step was a magical experience, glowing with his love for her.

The moon turned to gold as it lifted higher, creating a flight of golden steps coming closer and closer to them. They're for us, Christabel thought—the staircase to a golden future together. And she rested her head on Jared's shoulder, and knew she didn't need anything else. She had everything she wanted in the man who held her.

"I love you so much, Jared," she whispered. "Thank you for rescuing me and making this happen. All of it. You, me, Alicia..."

"Oh, I was only thinking of my pleasure," he teased. "After all, it is my pleasure to love you."

She smiled, her heart singing at the thought of going to bed with her *husband* tonight. Her true husband in every sense. The staircase to the moon was wonderful, but nothing—her mind flitted through the exquisite memories Jared had already given her, her

body instantly zinging with anticipation of so much
more to come—absolutely nothing, she thought bliss-
fully, could be more wonderful than being *the pleasure King's bride*!

*An electric chemistry with a disturbingly
familiar stranger...
A reawakening of passions long forgotten...
And a compulsive desire to get to know
this stranger all over again!*

Because

**What the memory has lost,
the body never forgets**

In Harlequin Presents®
over the coming months look out for:

BACK IN THE MARRIAGE BED
by Penny Jordan
On sale September, #2129

SECRET SEDUCTION
by Susan Napier
On sale October, #2135

THE SICILIAN'S MISTRESS
by Lynne Graham
On sale November, #2139

Available wherever Harlequin books are sold.

HARLEQUIN®
Makes any time special ™

Visit us at www.eHarlequin.com   HPAMN

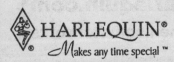
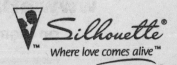

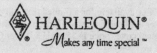

HARLEQUIN

Duets™